A HAND ON MY SHOULDER

By the same authors

Guidelines for Today:
The Ten Commandments in a Modern Context

A HAND ON MY SHOULDER

*True stories of how God communicates
with us today*

NORAH COOK and VERA FRAMPTON

NEW CHERWELL PRESS · OXFORD

First published in Great Britain 1995
by New Cherwell Press
7 Mount Street, Oxford OX2 6DH
Copyright © 1995 N. Cook and V. Frampton

British Library Cataloguing-in-Publication Data
A catalogue record for this book is available
from the British Library

ISBN 1-900312-00-X

Cover design by Philip Carr
Cover photograph by Zefa
Printed in Malta by Interprint

CONTENTS

Preface

How far is God known? How far is God knowable? Such questions were put so often to a school chaplain that he decided a book on the subject was needed. He wrote to Norah Cook, author of *Guidelines for Today: the Ten Commandments in a Modern Context*, to ask if she and her co-author Vera Frampton would consider preparing such a book. *A Hand on my Shoulder* is the result.

Today there is an upsurge of interest in spiritual questions. Tired of materialism, more and more people, particularly the young, are looking elsewhere both for inner satisfaction and for an answer to what has come to be called 'the moral maze'.

If there is a God, are there means of communication between that God and us, whatever our age and background? Apart from what we may have to say to him in our prayers and requests, what does he have to say to us?

This is a book of true stories of ordinary people and the ways in which they believe God has intervened in their lives, sometimes in moments of crisis or despair, at times inspiring them to acts of courage and leadership, of which they would never have thought themselves capable.

The stories are told by people from different parts of the world. For some, the art of communicating with a source of more than human wisdom was learned through a friend, through circumstances, through a Bible passage or a church service. Often communication seems to have come through a thought so unexpected, yet so persistent, that the person receiving it could only say, like young Samuel in the Old Testament, 'Speak, Lord, your servant is listening' – and then put the thought into action.

In some of the stories the term 'the inner voice' is mentioned to describe the source of direction. A 'still, small voice' is a phrase found in the Bible and much in use today.

The book was originally conceived with young people in mind. The most enlightening and encouraging part of the preparation came from discussions in schools with third and sixth year students on the question: 'Do you think that God can and does communicate with us?'

The schools included Colston's Collegiate and Monks Park, Bristol. We would like to thank Edward J. Elsey, Chaplain of Colston's, and Beverley Oldfield, former Head of Religious Education at Monks Park, for their co-operation.

Some of the students' comments have been included in the introductory notes to the different sections of stories which have been grouped according to content. Ages are approximate and names fictitious. Each story is followed by suggested questions for discussion.

It was the Rev. Richard Ballard, Chaplain of Westminster School, who, as indicated, gave the original suggestion for the book. He has been consulted from the start on key points. Jackie Sherlock, Religious Education Consultant, has given us throughout the benefit of her considerable experience in teaching Religious Studies. The manuscript was read by her and by Sydney Cook, both of whom raised valuable points.

We are grateful to them and to all who have had a part in this venture.

NORAH COOK
VERA FRAMPTON

1. NATURE, POETRY AND WORSHIP

Nature speaks to some people of God, the Creator. They take time to look and think, and feel joy and perhaps sadness, expressing their emotions in art, poetry and music.

A consciousness of the beauty of nature is more likely in the open spaces of the countryside, where there may be more time to reflect and gaze on the wonder of the sun, moon and stars and ever-changing panorama of the skies.

In many urban areas there are trees, green squares and parks, and often unexpected small gardens. Busy, crowded cities do not offer such refreshment. As plants struggle for the light through the crannies of shattered walls on derelict sites, so everywhere the human spirit reaches out to something or Someone beyond, 'the one True Light that lighteth all people.' One poet wrote of how this caused him to reflect upon God:

> Flower in the crannied wall,
> I pluck you out of the crannies.
> I hold you here, root and all, in my hand,
> Little flower – but if I could understand
> What you are, root and all, and all in all,
> I should know what God and man is.
>
> *Alfred, Lord Tennyson*

Two students who were asked 'How are you aware of what you call God?' gave the following replies:

> **Every now and then I come across something, possibly a feature of nature or a beautiful sight, and although I am an avid scientist, I do not believe science explains it all. There must be something else, and it is in this that I see touches of God.** James, 13

I am aware of what I call God by church buildings and gatherings, answers to some of my prayers, help in difficult situations, books like the Bible and sometimes church sermons. Pictures, icons, stained glass windows that depict God also make me more aware of him.

Martin, 13

STORIES

Escaped as a Bird
Experiencing God Through Nature
In Praise of the Creator
A Hand on my Shoulder

Psalm 118:5-6

Escaped as a Bird

Escaped as a bird
From the web of pain;
Finding the solace
In a glad refrain.   W.F.

Nagata Honami, son of a Japanese farmer, had an exciting future ahead of him. Right from the start his father encouraged him to study hard to become qualified to take his place in a new and changing Japan, where science and technology were all-important to compete with Western Civilisation. While still at primary school he was eager to prepare for this by studying. Then the blow struck. He had contracted leprosy, a terrible, disfiguring disease which, although curable today, still grips some people with fear and causes sufferers to be isolated and rejected by their community.

Nagata, a brilliant, sensitive boy, at first tried to kill himself. When the government opened the leprosy colony at Oshima he set out for a life of exile, with great bitterness. In his suffering and despair Jesus Christ became real to him. This gave him new hope and purpose.

Though badly injured and partly blind, he became the cheerful, shining spirit of the colony. He welcomed new patients, played with the children and kept up the morale of the very ill. It was as though he had escaped from the sufferings of his body into a different realm.

He began to express himself in the short, poignant poems of which the Japanese are so fond, and inspired others to write them. Instead of being broken on the anvil of pain, suffering and deformity, these sufferers have found faith, peace and joy through the loving care shown by members of the Leprosy Mission and American Leprosy Missions.

3

A selection of their poems was first published in Tokyo, Japan, by American Leprosy Missions under the title of *Souls Undaunted*. The art of Japanese poetry is to present a picture in a few lines by concentrating on image and suggestion. These poems are written in Haiku, a traditional Japanese style, and were translated into English by Walter Fawcett of the Leprosy Mission and published by them. The story is taken from the introduction.

The following poems show the writers' awareness of God in nature:

> I do not fear to tread the road
>   I cannot see.
> Because the hand of One Who loves
>   Is leading me.
>
>   Nagata

> Worship I God in song.
>   Gladly my lips shall cry
> Praise from my inmost heart
>   Until my bones do lie
> Under the sands of Oshima,
>   Under its shining sky.
>
>   Nagata

> The evening sea reflects the hills of gold,
>   The soul of autumn hovers in the air,
> We watch your boat glide silently away
>   And for you breathe to God a grateful prayer.
>
>   Nagata

4

I wander to a little pine-clad hill
  Above the sea
  For prayer;
And every dawn I find a nightingale
  Is singing there.

Mumei

  My hands are numb and broken,
    I am blind;
  And I can neither feel nor see
    My little pot of violets;
    So I bend to kiss
    The wee, sweet flowers
That mean so much to me.

Mumei

    I know Thou art
    When sudden prayer
    Wells all unbidden
    In my humble heart.

Kawabuchi

QUESTIONS AND TASKS

1. You are Nagata: describe how you felt before and after your spiritual experience.

2. How did Nagata act after his experience?

3. Why did Nagata no longer fear the future?

4. Illustrate one of these poems.

Experiencing God through Nature

Many find that God communicates with them through art and through nature. Here is what Heaton Cooper, well-known Lakeland artist, wrote.

'One summer evening, when I was seventeen, I was up on Wansfell above the head of Windermere, trying to paint the valley of the Brathay that was crowned by some of the highest and most rugged of our mountains. But, after struggling for some hours, I had to admit complete failure, so I stopped and just looked. The wind was coming from the sea some thirty miles to the west. It was bringing clouds which, when they reached the mountains, were sending down moving curtains of rain. I saw the streams and rivers bringing water into the lake which bore it back again into the sea. Something about this orderly cycle of the movement of moisture brought to me an intense awareness that I was seeing part of the design of the whole universe, and with it came the conviction that there was a mind, therefore a person, who was creating this design. And because a person, somehow I, also a person, could become part of this design if I chose to.

'The vivid sense of joy and ecstasy left me in no doubt about choosing. The glow of this experience lasted for several days, and has recurred on many occasions since, though not quite so overwhelmingly as it did on the first occasion.

'This was my first experience of the presence of God in nature. On reading Psalm 104, some of the writings of Chinese painters and philosophers, and some of the earlier poems of William Wordsworth, I saw that others had had similar experiences of the divine spirit in nature. Some had been content to have this as the inspiration of their life and work. Others had gone on to discover God becoming man in the person of Jesus Christ.'

QUESTIONS AND TASKS

1. Illustrate what the artist saw as he looked at the valley.

2. What awareness came to Heaton Cooper as he watched the movement of the winds and clouds, streams, rivers and lakes?

3. Make a list of things in nature which you find beautiful. Draw them if you wish, or write a poem about one of them, even a leaf or piece of fruit.

4. What do you think natural beauty can tell us about God?

5. What choice was Heaton Cooper faced with? What influenced his choice?

In Praise of the Creator

Bless the Lord, O my soul. O Lord my God, thou art very great: thou art clothed with honour and majesty.

Who coverest thyself with light as with a garment: who stretcheth the heavens like a curtain.

He sendeth the springs into the valleys, which run among the hills.

They give drink to every beast of the field: the wild asses quench their thirst.

By them shall the fowls of the air have their habitation, which sing among the branches.

He watereth the hills from his chambers: the earth is satisfied with the fruit of thy works.

He causeth the grass to grow for the cattle, and herb for the service of man: that he may bring forth food out of the earth.

The hills are a refuge for the wild goats: and the rocks for the conies.

O Lord, how manifold are thy works! In wisdom hast thou made them all: the earth is full of thy riches.

The glory of the Lord shall endure for ever: the Lord shall rejoice in his works.

He looketh on the earth and it trembleth: he toucheth the hills and they smoke.

I will sing unto the Lord as long as I live: I will sing praises to my God while I have my being.

My meditation of him shall be sweet: I will be glad in the Lord.

From *Psalm 104*

We praise Thee with our thoughts, O God.
We praise Thee even as the sun praises Thee in
    the morning.
May we find joy in being Thy servants.

Keep us under Thy protection.
Forgive our sins and give us Thy love.

God made the rivers to flow.
They feel no weariness; they cease not from flowing.
They fly swiftly like birds in the air.

May the stream of my life flow into the rivers
    of righteousness
Loose the bonds of sun that bind me;
Let not the thread of my song be cut while I sing;
and let not my work end before its fulfilment.

From the *Rig Veda*, 11.28, a Hindu Hymn

Praise be to him who, when I call on him,
Answers me, slow though I am when he calls me.
Praise be to him who gives to me when I ask him
Miserly though I am when he asks a loan of me.
My Lord I praise, for he is of my praise most worth.

From an Islamic source

TASK
Write a poem about God the Creator, or describe some of the
things he does, according to these readings.

A Hand on my Shoulder

'God does not exist. Only silly, ignorant old women believe in Him.' These and other arguments had been drummed into Irina, aged ten, and her class for an hour during the period for atheist instruction. It had all got so boring. Why, if God did not exist, did people spend so much time talking about Him? It made Irina think that perhaps He did exist.

Irina was born in the Ukraine, then part of the USSR. The Communist Government's policy at that time was to eradicate belief in God. Bibles and other religious books were banned.

She began to talk to God secretly. This is how she describes it: 'At first I only ask endless questions. On His side, God makes no attempt to appear to me personally in a blaze of light, or anything like that, or even answer my questions audibly. Yet the answers come, all the same: either a book with the answer turns up next day, or I suddenly feel an inward certainty about the right reply to this or that question . . .

'The atheist's favourite argument that, if God existed, He would not let children die in wars, and suchlike, cuts no ice with me. If we the people start wars knowing full well that innocents perish in them, what right have we to reproach God for granting us free will? If I am robbed and get my throat cut tomorrow, is it God's fault? No, if He's really kind and all-powerful, He'll take me to Him and I'll be much better off than in school or on the streets.'

Once the class was throwing horse chestnuts at each other in the teacher's absence, when one fell into an inkwell and smashed it. Ink splashed against the wall. The pupils began to leave the room rapidly. The teacher returned, appalled at the mess. 'Who did it?' she enquired of Irina. Irina made one excuse after another for not knowing the culprit. The next pupil asked merely said, 'I'm not going to answer you.' What courage! This made Irina feel badly at telling lies; surely there would have been another way not to split on her friends. She resolved never to tell lies again. She felt ashamed of being so afraid of people who get angry and shout at you. What a spineless creature she was to be so intimidated. She decided to think a lot and talk to God more, then nobody would be able to manipulate her. This decision was to stand her in good stead later.

Irina had several friends, including Igor. He was born with deformed feet and might never be able to walk properly. After an operation he had to wear first plaster and then orthopaedic boots which made it impossible to run or jump about, so in the end he discarded them, and began to use his legs, though this was very painful. A friend gave him some physical training and he even learned to box so as to be able to stand up to a school bully.

After school, Irina went to Odessa University, while Igor was studying to be a thermal physicist like his father. When they met again Igor was a handsome young man of seventeen. They had much to talk to each other about, and would sometimes tease each other.

One day Igor told Irina how he had come to believe in God. He said, 'There had to be a beginning of some kind for our world; that stands to reason. An impulse and meaning.' They discussed this meaning and began to realise that they had come to believe in God along different paths but had reached an identical understanding. Both had learned of the fine line that distinguishes 'good' from 'bad' and between 'honour' and 'dishonour'. Then Igor said, 'Has it happened to you that the answer to some problem has come as if out of nowhere? As if you have been guided by an invisible hand on your shoulder?' 'Yes,' replied Irina. 'And it was always the right solution, one which you never had to regret?' 'Why, yes. Has it happened to you too?' 'Yes. And I know what's behind it.'

Igor qualified and got a job at his father's institute. An anonymous complaint was that the father had used undue influence. This was not true, but one of them would have to resign. Igor was younger with more chance of getting a job, so he did; he got another job as engineer in the Steel Foundry Institute. Meantime Irina too was working.

On her 25th birthday came a knock at the door and there stood Igor, dripping wet from the rain, with a dark red rose for Irina. He had come to ask her to be his wife. Irina hesitated. How would they live, and what about her teaching job in Odessa? However, Igor went ahead and found a temporary flat for them in Kiev, and later they married.

Life under Communist rule became increasingly difficult for many people. If you did not toe the line and say as the authorities ordered, you might be arrested and imprisoned. Irina and Igor decided to follow the dictates of conscience. They could not stand by while others suffered, and so became part of an underground network, printing and distributing forbidden books, including the poems Irina wrote. They were an expression of freedom of thinking. She was more likely than Igor to be arrested, because of her poetry.

Irina had a great fear of being shut in, so Igor helped her to get used to closed-in places by going into lifts and the underground.

Irina is arrested
In September 1982 Irina, aged twenty-eight, was arrested and charged with 'anti-soviet agitation and propaganda'. Her crime was 'manufacture and dissemination of her poems'. After some months she was sentenced to seven years hard labour and five years internal exile.

Igor was allowed a visit to his wife. She recited all the poems she had been writing. Twenty-four hours after Igor's return to Moscow, all the information about her hard treatment in prison and the poems were typed and on their way to England. Igor was not allowed another visit for three years and his letters to her were kept back. But somehow her writings were smuggled out and sent abroad.

By this time several countries were producing translations of her poems and knew of her sufferings. Intensive campaigns were launched on her behalf and many letters were sent to the Soviet Ambassador in London, her Prison Governor and Prosecutor. In May 1986 a book was published in England entitled *No, I'm not afraid* containing her poems and articles about her.

The prison authorities now made repeated attempts to persuade Irina to admit her guilt and ask for clemency. 'Never,' she said.

Igor loved his wife dearly and suffered greatly at not being able to see her. The KGB urged him to write an appeal on Irina's behalf telling him that otherwise Irina, who was seriously ill, would die.

'Igor wrestled within himself to reach a decision. And the answer seemed to come from somewhere . . . outside himself: 'Not a line. All will be well.' He stopped in wonder, feeling a touch of the Divine Hand on his shoulder. He had experienced it before and felt no further qualms.'

Eventually, with pressure from the West and a more liberal attitude in Russia, Irina was released in October 1986. At last she and Igor were together again. How thin she was! In December they came to England and were warmly welcomed by friends as they arrived in London.

Irina received much-needed medical treatment. When she had recovered there was a crowded Service of Thanksgiving in February 1987 led by the Bishops of Birmingham and Aston, when some of her poems were read. Five years later it was announced in the newspapers that, despite being told in prison that she would never be able to have any children, Irina Ratushinskaya had given birth to twin sons.

Here is a poem by Irina Ratushinskaya read out at the Service:

BELIEVE ME

Believe me, it was often thus:
In solitary cells, on winter nights
A sudden sense of joy and warmth
And a resounding note of love.
And then, unsleeping, I would know
A-huddle by an icy wall:
Someone is thinking of me now,
Petitioning the Lord for me.
My dear ones, thank you all
Who did not falter, who believed in us!
In the most fearful prison hour
We probably would not have passed
Through everything — from end to end,
Our heads held high, unbowed —
Without your valiant hearts
To light our pain.

QUESTIONS AND TASKS

1. Some books, including the Bible, were banned when Russia was under Communist rule. Why do you think that was?

2. Put down on paper any thoughts you have about God, as Irina did.

3. Design a poster drawing attention to Irina's sufferings, giving a brief outline of them and some suggestions for action to be taken.

4. What were Irina's fears? How did she overcome them?

2. THE LISTENERS

God sometimes gives a person a compelling thought about their own or someone else's need.

In the following stories the people concerned listened to and obeyed these thoughts. The results show how important they can be.

Below are some comments from students about God's existence and how he communicates with us:

> **I believe God is here, not in the large changes, the revolutions and massacres, but in the little things that make up a normal man's life.** Mark, 13

> **God seems to be in most things I do. I feel him most when doing something dangerous or difficult. By this I mean travelling or feeling upset. I feel a voice, as it were, inside me telling me to look at it from a different perspective.** Charles, 13

> **He gives you a feeling. He gets inside your mind.**
> Duncan, 13

STORIES
Moment of Truth
Saved by a Safety Helmet
'I hate this dump!'
Strange Direction

John 10:27

Moment of Truth

There were many times when Pat found that God was there when she needed him. She believes that if you love God you obey the thoughts he gives. Early in her life she decided to obey in matters big and small.

Soon afterwards the decision was put to the test. Her boss asked her to arrange for a French girl to come to England for a month's experience in the firm's office in the northern outskirts of London.

On the day of the expected arrival, Pat was just setting out for Victoria Station to meet the girl when an unexpected thought came into her mind to buy some flowers first and leave them as a welcome in the digs she had arranged.

'No,' she said to herself, 'I've done enough already in making all the arrangements for her stay.' However, the thought wouldn't go away. Somewhat against her will, Pat bought the flowers.

When she arrived at the digs, the door was opened by the landlady in a state of great agitation. She was at that very moment taking a phone call from the Newhaven emigration authorities. They had detained the French girl because she had no work permit, as was required at that time, and were going to send her back to France. Pat took over the phone call and was able to explain to the authorities the special circumstances of the girl's short-stay visit. The authorities were satisfied and all was well.

If Pat hadn't called when she did, the girl would have been turned back, her visit denied – and incidentally Pat would have been left waiting in vain at the station.

Pat, who is now elderly, says this was for her a moment of truth about the importance of heeding the 'inner voice', which has stood her in good stead ever since.

16

QUESTIONS AND TASKS

1. What do you think is meant by 'the inner voice'?

2. Why was her experience of 'the inner voice' so important in Pat's life?

3. You are the French girl. Describe what happened on arrival at Newhaven, your anxiety and then relief at the phone call.

Saved by a Safety Helmet

Ever since she was a little girl Jenny, an Australian, had turned to Jesus when she was in any difficulty. Once when she was eight years old she went to a summer camp with her friends. They all went for a trip on a small steam train. Jenny was not one to push herself forward, and by the time she got out of the train the others had all gone, and she was left standing alone on the platform. There she was in a strange place, where she knew no one. Yet step by step she was shown what to do and where to go, until at last she was reunited with her party.

On leaving school she wanted to study medicine, but missed out by a couple of marks in her exams. So she started on science, hoping to do well enough to transfer later into medicine.

Jenny used to ride her bicycle to the university. On the last day of the academic year when she came out of one of her lectures she found it had been raining and her safety helmet was full of water, so she didn't want to put it on. But then she had the clear thought that she must put it on, which she did – drips and all. On her way home she tried to cross a very busy highway. There were two cars coming, but she could only see one of them. She hurried to pass the first car, and went head first through the window of the second. Her helmet was broken, so she would not be alive today if she had not been wearing it.

Jenny missed all her study week with concussion, and even on the day before her first exam she was unable to hold a normal discussion with a friend. She came out of those examinations with three High Distinctions and a Credit! She had done her work throughout the year and felt that somehow God had helped her to concentrate and think clearly during the exams. Because of these results she was accepted into one of the only two medical schools in Australia which were part of large hospitals and where they had contact with patients from the first term in their first year. This was exactly what she wanted.

QUESTIONS AND TASKS

1. Draw a sketch of how the road accident happened. *Or* describe it: 'My name is Jenny . . .'

2. How do you think Jenny's early faith may have helped her in later life?

3. Have you ever been protected from harm by a strong feeling? How do you account for this?

4. If you wish, write a true or fictitious story about such a situation.

Acts 5:32 (2nd part)

'I hate this dump!'

Barry Kiswell opened his Sunday paper and settled down to read it. His attention was caught by a story headlined 'Michelle's home is a shop doorway', with a photograph. The story was about the plight of homeless youngsters sleeping rough in London. A reporter had come across Michelle, who said to him, 'I hate this dump! I cry myself to sleep.'

As he read about her and other young people, he had the growing conviction that the Holy Spirit was telling him to go to London and meet them. His wife, Mary, suggested he took flasks of home-made vegetable soup. So, late that evening, he and a friend, Arthur, set off for London, to the Strand, a long road which had been mentioned in the story. Near the top of the Strand were a group of people in a large shop doorway. He felt sure this was the place to stop. The teenagers, huddled under a blanket, welcomed a cup of hot soup. Presently he looked up and there was Michelle. She wanted to talk.

Michelle said that on her sixteenth birthday she had gone to a disco with a friend. At the end of the evening they had been kidnapped by two men who brought them to London where they were imprisoned for two months and physically abused. Eventually they escaped and had lived on the streets for four months.

She kept asking if Barry believed her. He said he did and asked why she had not contacted her parents. 'They'd think I was making it up,' she replied. Michelle asked if he could arrange for her to return home and gave him her parents' telephone number.

The next morning he telephoned the number. A man answered. Barry said he believed he had been talking with his daughter. He was told that his daughter had disappeared six months earlier and he and his wife had heard nothing since, although a nationwide alert had been put out by the police.

20

Next day Barry and Arthur returned to London. At first they drew a blank. They settled down on the pavement to talk with a group of alcoholics when suddenly Michelle appeared. She was overjoyed when Barry said he had been talking to her parents and that they loved her and wanted her home. He offered to collect her the following Friday at 7 a.m.

When he arrived he gave the little group hot tea. Michelle said farewell and off they set. At first they went to Barry's home where his wife was waiting with a hot breakfast. Then they went on their way.

Her parents gave Michelle a great welcome. Barry told them how his finding her had come about. As practising Catholics her parents had prayed for her every day, supported by their parish priest who had prayed every Sunday in church for Michelle.

Barry said that this episode had been a lesson in learning to hear and obey the promptings of the Holy Spirit. This discernment comes through time spent alone with God and being available to him. It was one of the major factors in the rapid expansion of Christianity in its early days.

QUESTIONS AND TASKS

1. List the key points in the story which led to Michelle being found and returning home.

2. You are Michelle's mother. Describe to a church friend what happened to your daughter.

3. Draw Michelle in her 'dump'.

4. What do you think Barry meant by 'being available to God?' How does his story illustrate this?

Strange Direction

Dr Vaughan had several experiences of God's guidance, sometimes when he had asked about something. At other times a thought would come unexpectedly and he would act on it, without knowing why.

On one occasion he and his wife Freda had rented a house in a Melbourne suburb in Australia for a holiday. One afternoon, after lunch in the city, Freda went off to do some shopping. Dr Vaughan was wondering what to do, when he had a very clear direction: 'Go back to the house.' As he hesitated, the thought came again, so he went back. There was no one about as he let himself into the house and he felt completely mystified.

Then came a knock at the door. He opened it to a shabbily dressed man who asked, 'Can I have a gardening job to do?' Dr Vaughan was about to say they were only renting the house for a holiday, when he noticed how unhappy the man looked, and found him a job to do. When it was done, he paid the man and invited him in to have a cup of tea.

The doctor noticed that his hands were quite smooth, and certainly not those of a gardener. So he said, 'You aren't really a gardener, are you?' 'No,' replied the man. 'I lost my job as an accountant when the firm cut down on staff, and I have tramped all over Melbourne trying to get work, with no success.' He paused and, looking at the doctor, said, 'I asked you for a job as I have decided to end it all and wanted the fare to go down to St Kilda and jump in.' St Kilda is one of Melbourne's harbours.

The doctor asked him more about himself. The man said he had had a Christian faith when young, but when he grew older he forgot it, and now he had none. The doctor said, 'You may have forgotten God, but he has not forgotten you,' and went on to tell him how God had directed him so strangely to return to the house so that he would be there when the man called. His caller was very affected by this. How could he end his life in view of what he had just been told?

Dr Vaughan got in touch with a friend to see if he could help, and he was able to find employment for the man.

QUESTIONS AND TASKS

1. What made the unemployed man change his mind about committing suicide?

2. Write to someone about the visit to the doctor as if you were the unemployed man: 'I was unemployed and desperate . . .'

3. What suggestions can you offer to help unemployed people?

3. TIGHT CORNERS

We all get into difficulties at times. When we do, most of us pray, perhaps only then. Or maybe someone else prays for us. Things don't always work out as we would like, and maybe some day we will understand.

In the following stories God showed his care by answering prayer in remarkable ways.

Here are some views expressed by students:

> **I don't know whether I believe in God, but he's helped me out of some pretty tight squeezes.**
>
> Colin, 13

> **I'm an atheist, till something goes wrong in my life.**
>
> Edward, 13

> **You pray, and God makes things happen.**
>
> Aisha, 13

> **I'm an agnostic. My personal idea of God is a way of explaining the inexplicable.**
>
> William, 13

STORIES   Guardian Angel
Snowy
Doug and his O.C.

24

Guardian Angel

Before Rhodesia became Zimbabwe by peaceful means under black majority rule on 18 April 1980 there was intense guerilla warfare. No white farms were safe, and intensive security was necessary. This remarkable story is set in those times.

On arriving at her parents' farm in a dangerous area of Salisbury, Rhodesia, Elspeth discovered to her dismay that her parents had gone away for the night. She felt afraid but busied herself with chores until it grew dark. Just as darkness fell she found to her horror that she had left her washing outside on the line. It was dangerous to leave it all night as it would let any wandering guerrillas think the farm was deserted, but it was even more dangerous to go out into the darkness. What should she do? She prayed for help and direction and God gave her a very clear thought: 'Go out and get the washing in as quickly as possible and keep praying all the time.'

She did this and got back inside without incident. The night passed peacefully, but next morning a security patrol arrived and asked anxiously if she was safe. Was she disturbed during the night? When she said she had not been, they appeared amazed. 'Then who was with you last night?' they asked. She replied that she had been quite alone. The officer then told her that they had captured some guerillas who said they had been about to attack her home after dark the previous night and were watching from nearby bushland. Then they had seen her come out to take the washing and with her was an armed man, and the whole scene was brilliantly lit. She had been conversing with him all the while.

QUESTIONS AND TASKS

1. Discuss in pairs Elspeth's predicament, what she decided to do and what her action showed, then report back.

2. Illustrate what happened when Elspeth got the washing in, according to the guerillas.

3 Sometimes people refer to their 'guardian angels'. What do you think they mean by that?

4. What do you imagine guardian angels are like?

Snowy

Snowy Mohala from South Africa describes
her long struggle with drug addiction

At the age of 16 I insisted on marrying against my parents'
wishes. Soon we realised it was a mistake and the marriage
packed up. But there were two children involved, a boy and a girl.

During the divorce hearing I refused to appear in court
because I knew there was no way I could look after our children
if I got custody of them. My husband gave the children to his
parents.

I took to alcohol and drugs for consolation. I just wanted to
drown my pain and continue living as if nothing had changed. I
could not go back to my parents because I had disobeyed them.

The streets became my home. I sometimes slept in drinking
houses, usually alive with music. I was hooked on marijuana and
'madrass', a tablet I used to take daily. Life was lonely and I
suffered a great deal, especially as I knew that what I was doing
was wrong – but I just could not help myself.

One day I decided to write to my father and plead with him
to take me back. He did not reply. After a while I telephoned to
apologise for the pain and disgrace I had caused him.

Deep in my heart I was tired of that kind of life. So I persisted
with the phone calls to my father. Eventually he agreed to have
me back, but only to live in an outer room and not in the main
house with the rest of the family. I went home. It was a small
room with no window except a big uncovered hole. I felt hurt and
rejected but I knew it was the price I had to pay for the way I had
chosen to live.

I feel my father could have treated me better, but I was
fortunate to have a younger sister who cared enough to help me
get free of my addictions.

One morning I saw an old school friend. I called out to her in excitement by the nickname which we used at school. She looked, came closer but could not make out who I was. When I told her she burst into tears and almost immediately turned away. She only believed it was me because I was the only Snowy in my area.

When I told my father what had happened he said, 'I have been waiting and praying for this day for a long time now.' He brought out a photo of me and asked me to hold it next to my face and look in the mirror. Beside my photo I saw an old granny – it could have been two different people.

Suddenly I had a sense that God was there. Nobody told me what to do. I locked myself in my room and prayed as I had never done before. While I prayed I felt a movement in my room and as soon as I opened my eyes I saw that my room was dirty and the blanket smelled horrible. I opened the door and immediately started airing, clearing and cleaning the room. For the first time in many years I felt clean.

A few months later I got a job, and eventually bought a house. Then I went for my children.

Now the family relationships are healing in all directions and I can communicate with people again. I decided to use my experience to help other people who are following the road I once walked. Many people are responding. If I could change, then surely others can too.

QUESTIONS AND TASKS

1. Draw any event in Snowy's life or dramatise it.

2. What made Snowy see herself as she had become?

3. What do you think was the movement in the room?

4. What actions did she take to rehabilitate herself after her strange experience?

5. a) Do you think her father was very unkind?
   b) Why do you think he wouldn't help her any more than he did?

Doug and his O.C.

Doug Walter was a stocky, shortish man, very determined and with a great sense of humour. He was called up in the Second World War and trained as a despatch driver in the Royal Army Service Corps and sent with an ambulance unit to the Middle East. He was asked to look after a young lieutenant, his O.C.

The O.C. was often amused by this unusual little man, but came to respect his habit of reading the Bible and praying each day, expecting God to give him direction or 'guidance' as he called it.

On one occasion the unit was ordered to pack up and leave Alexandria. The route lay across a vast desert. At first there were small villages and Army and RAF camps, but these became less frequent until suddenly all signs of civilisation ended. There was nothing except scrub and churned-up dirt tracks made by Italians advancing and the British driving them back.

One track they followed ended abruptly and they could see only some tyre marks. They were quite lost, and panic set in. The O.C., who was driving, began to go faster over all the lumps and depressions and as the vehicle rocked, howls of protest came from the back. When Doug suggested going more slowly and trying to find a map reference, the O.C. got really mad. He shouted at Doug, 'You're always talking about God's guidance. Why don't you try to get some now?' 'All right, if you'll only shut up for a minute, I'll try,' replied Doug, losing *his* temper.

A short, rather cross silence followed; then Doug prayed for direction. He looked at the horizon — still nothing. Then something caught his eye, a kind of twinkle. Perhaps it was the sun catching in an empty petrol can far away in the distance.

'Aim for that twinkle,' said Doug.

The O.C. swung the truck hard over, to a great roar from behind. They reached the top of an unsuspected slight undulation and from there, on the skyline, they could see a line of makeshift telegraph poles with a wire on them. Civilisation! Sure enough these led to a signals camp. They were lent a tent for the night, given food and in the morning told the way to go.

Last thing that night, when Doug had said his very grateful prayers, the O.C. came in and said to everyone, 'You know, we were lost today, and it's thanks to Doug's praying that we're here.'

Doug says in his book *Some Soldier!* 'It is because of incidents like this that I believe anyone sincerely trying to be obedient to the will of God can receive direction, in big things and in everyday things.'

QUESTIONS AND TASKS

1. You are one of the soldiers at the back of the truck when it got lost. Write home and describe what happened.

2. How did Doug find the way to go? Was he just lucky or was it something more?

3. Draw a scene from the story.

4. What condition does Doug list as needed for receiving direction from God? When should one seek it?

4. A BIGGER AIM

We live in a fast-changing world. Advances in science and technology are bringing many benefits. They also pose some new threats.

The dividing line between right and wrong has become blurred. In a highly competitive world the importance of the individual is often ignored. It is a bewildering time in which to grow up. While many young people are keen to help others and have high ideals, others may drift into crime or drug-taking, or seek questionable ways of making money.

Sometimes a total change of attitude is needed, a radical re-think of one's life. These three stories are examples of this.

An African journalist set out to make a lot of money by becoming a popular gossip columnist. She became unhappy when she started to think about the effects her writings were having. She turned to God and found a better way to use her talents.

A girl of mixed ethnic background felt confused, not knowing where she belonged. Friends told her God had a plan for her life as she was. This brought peace and freedom.

Two young West Indians had experiences in prison which changed their lives and set them on a new road.

Here are some students' comments during a discussion which seem apt:

Certain aspects of society go against what God would want . . . Today education is geared towards helping you make money. People lose their sense of direction, as I feel I am losing mine.

Alistair, 18

We come to the stage when we scrap the values of our parents and adopt those of society.

Sheila, 15

I'm interested in friends helping you find the right course when you have to make decisions.

Jennifer, 17

STORIES

Money isn't Everything
Identity Crisis
A Better Way

Money isn't Everything

Choice Okoro, who lives in Nigeria, went into journalism because she felt it was the only way in which she could become rich and famous. She felt that wealth and fame were the only means by which her generation would rise above the corruption and poverty so evident in society today.

After completing a compulsory year with the National Youth Service Corps, she marched into the offices of the biggest newspaper in Nigeria. So confident was she in her great potential that she got them to take her on, and soon proved herself. She had a nose for the malicious stories that people love to read. She also had a knack of exposing the secrets of well-known people, and frequented the most exclusive night-clubs to gather the material.

The stories she wrote increased the circulation of the magazines, and within eighteen months she was in great demand. Her life was not satisfying, but she felt it would get better once she got to the top.

Out of curiosity Choice Okoro attended a 'Creators of Peace' meeting organised by African women in Lagos. She intended spending about an hour there, but stayed the whole day.

She began to realise how the victims of her gossip columns felt, and decided she could no longer continue writing them. It was not easy. Her editors did not like the new Choice Okoro with her changed attitudes. Eventually she knew that she had to resign if she intended to start afresh. She then got a job as deputy editor in a smaller newspaper. It used to have nude photographs but after a persistent struggle she convinced everyone that they were not necessary, and the photographs were dropped. The readership increased as a result.

Choice now has more satisfying friendships. She realises that self-worth comes from inside and not from other people's assessment of you. This was her first taste of true freedom. The release of her creative talents led to her writing and producing a musical, with other Nigerian women, with the aim of challenging young people to be more responsible for their country and its future.

Asked what part God had in the changes in her life, Choice Okoro wrote: 'All these changes were brought about by God. I had felt too small to have any involvement with him. When I realised from the "Creators of Peace" meeting that God has a plan for everybody's life, including mine, I began to open my heart to him. It was refreshing to think that God the Almighty could notice me and guide me in the minute details of my life. I need no longer be pulled by demands from friends, peer group, money and my job, but answerable only to God; then I would be at peace with the world.

'At first I found it hard to live in a new way, because I had done a lot of things I felt guilty about. Later it became clear to me that I should first clean up my life. The more I did this, the more I understood that God had a new, better and bigger plan for me. So I accepted the challenge.'

QUESTIONS AND TASKS

1. What were the important things in Choice's life at that time?

2. You are Choice. Your conscience is bothering you. Write to your parents about your dilemma.

3. Choice felt under pressure. What realisation freed her and gave her peace of heart?

4. List some of the pressures people are under today.

5. Do you think journalists should write about people's personal lives? Why? or Why not?

Identity Crisis

The first turning point in the life of Linda Pierce, a secretary in Bombay, India, came at the age of thirteen. At a camp with people from different backgrounds and ethnic groups she heard someone say that God had a plan for her life. 'This was new and exciting,' she recalls. 'The small decisions I made then as a schoolgirl to be part of the "cure" and not the "disease" in India laid the foundations of my life.'

Linda belongs to the Anglo-Indian community and has Kashmiri, English, Irish and Armenian antecedents. Her family had always looked on themselves as Indians. Then one day, after a fight with another child, a neighbour told her that she did not fully belong to India and ought to live on the border. Linda was plagued by a crisis of identity.

She couldn't really blame people for thinking she came from some country other than India, but it hurt just the same. To feel that special sense of belonging became an important issue for her. She tried hard to look Indian and wore a sari.

She was nineteen and working voluntarily as a secretary to the director of a centre for reconciliation in Western India, when it dawned on her that she was spending her life trying to be someone else.

Linda realised that she could only love India as herself and that no one could take away that right. She felt a new freedom and peace. It didn't matter what she looked like any more. She even developed a sense of humour when fellow Indians asked her which country she came from.

Instead of hiding behind a wall she was now able to be honest about the hurt. She says, 'I knew the world needed an open-hearted person, not one who lived like an oyster in a hard shell. Imagine what a gift it was later to set foot in an English hamlet where my ancestors once lived, and to experience the beauty of

County Cork, Ireland, from where another branch of my family came.'

Over the last ten years she has edited a newsletter carrying stories of ordinary Indians whose decisions are making a difference to the quality of life in the village or on the factory floor.

QUESTIONS AND TASKS

1. Why did Linda have an identity crisis? How did she try to overcome it?

2. What key thought helped her to change her attitude?

3. You are a refugee. Your parents were killed and you were taken to a far country. You ask yourself 'who am I?' Write to a friend where you used to live and describe how you feel.

4. Draw Linda in an Indian costume.

A Better Way

Leonard Johnson is one of a large family who moved to England from Jamaica. He was expelled from school at fifteen, with no qualifications. He tried various jobs, but got involved with gangs and began to gamble, fight and shoplift. Eventually he was sent to prison for four years for burglary.

In prison Leonard began to read the Bible. He said, 'It was like a magnet. I kept coming back to it.' His conscience began to trouble him. One day he broke down and said to God, 'If you can change me, I'll give the rest of my life to helping other people.' He stopped smoking and receiving stolen goods when his friends visited him. After nineteen months he was let out on parole. Some of his friends cut up rough when he tried to join them, because of his change, but one understood. His name was Lawrence Fearon.

Lawrence's family had also come from Jamaica in the 1950s. He used to cause trouble at school and was sent to an approved school. He committed several offences and went to prison. There he noticed that many prisoners were middle-aged and decided he didn't want to end up like them.

On his release he was determined to settle back into the community without falling into his old bad habits. He met Leonard at a party in early 1981. They got talking. Leonard told Lawrence about his experience. This is how he put it: 'Life is like a whirlpool, with different boats swirling around in it. One boat is dancing and discoing. Another boat is seeing how smart you can look. Another is women, another is crime and another is fighting. The combination of all these was our life, but the whirlpool was dragging us under and we weren't noticing it. On the other side, however, was a shore, so I jumped out and swam to it to see what life was like there.' He went on to talk about his new-found beliefs and when Lawrence seemed to understand, he felt he had found an ally.

They began to speak at meetings. Leonard used to go into the pubs, bang a table and tell customers that there was a better way to live than by gambling, mugging and so on. More and more people turned up at meetings they held in homes, cafes and pubs. The time was ripe for the next move.

There was a converted underground car park used as the youth section of the only Council-run club in the area. They were given permission to use it. They cleaned the place up, painted it with lighter colours, got a sound system in for Friday nights and started a canteen. Soon it was a hive of activity.

Many of their ideas for helping the community came together in Spring 1981 when, with five others, they founded the Harlesden People's Community Council (HPCC). It was a grass-roots black community group. Courses were organised in drama, dancing, English, Bible Study and Black History.

'Inner City' riots

During that summer, riots broke out in several areas and began to spread towards theirs. Leonard tried to persuade youths not to join in. When violence began he asked the police for a few minutes to address the crowd. He told them how they had started to build something in the community and this was not the moment to destroy it all. People began dropping their weapons and drifting away.

The threatened riots alerted the Council to the needs of the community, and they began taking the work of the HPCC and its leaders more seriously. The Senior Social Worker encouraged them to prepare a document setting out all they felt was wrong. One of their recommendations was for a major community facility. Their present premises were now far too small.

The New Centre

Leonard heard of a huge empty bus garage up for sale at £2,000,000. Where could they find that sort of money? They would need to work with other bodies and lose some independence, but it was just what was needed.

Months went by without much happening, but Leonard never gave up. 'He was like Moses,' said Lawrence. He was sure that God had ordained it and that it was going to happen. The HPCC began to plan the new centre. Several government departments gave money grants and the bus garage was bought for £1,800,000.

Then began the work of cleaning and renovating the place. Young unemployed helped and were paid under a government scheme. The HPCC understood the running of the centre, helped by young offenders doing community work under supervision. The Manpower Services Commission helped and employment training was given under several heads.

As difficulties were overcome, the faith of Leonard and Lawrence was strengthened. They were invited to tell their story in other inner city areas. Lawrence said, 'We want most of all to show that people are capable of achieving responsibility and helping their deprived brothers. We want people to say: "If they can do that, maybe we can too."'

QUESTIONS AND TASKS

1. What effect did reading the Bible have on Leonard?

2. What made his friend Lawrence decide to give up crime?

3. Illustrate the whirlpool as Leonard described it, with a caption.

4. Evaluate in discussion or writing the social significance of the story.

5. RECONCILIATION

Today there is a marked increase in breakdowns in family life. There are many contributory factors to this. They always cause unhappiness, especially to the children.

Some couples seek counselling, and this may end in reconciliation. Others may divorce and then regret it later and remarry their partners.

In these two stories, where difficulties seemed insurmountable, those concerned turned to God. A new element entered into their lives and hope was born. With mutual apologies and forgiveness came a new understanding so that when disagreements arose again they could be resolved quickly.

The third story tells how a rebellious son of a famous father had a remarkable experience that eventually brought about a new relationship with his parents and friendship with a former enemy of his people. This played a vital part in ensuring that the transition to independence of an emerging nation was a peaceful one.

The following quotations include children's reactions to parents:

> **My parents quarrel terribly. I go away by myself and it calms me down.**
>
> Linda, 13

> **I think it is very important to find time to be on your own and to reflect on whatever has happened. Through that you confront your own memories and your own heart.**
>
> Peter, 16

Sometimes my mother and I shriek at each other. She says I don't do enough housework, and I have to do my homework. The Qur'an (Koran) says, 'Respect your father and your mother.'

Saleha, 13

STORIES

Divorce called off
'Don't let my parents split up'
'Now I call him brother'

Divorce called off

Bernard's and Joan's marriage was going to pieces. They decided to take a holiday abroad in the hope that it would help to mend their relationship. It didn't. Half way through, Joan packed her bags and returned home. She went to see a solicitor and started divorce proceedings. By the time Bernard arrived home, proceedings were well under way.

Bernard was extremely upset. He had turned a blind eye to the rising tension between himself and Joan, and marriage was a matter of principle for him. His family had been Catholics for generations. When they took the marriage vows and promised to be faithful to them, he meant it. 'Till death do us part' meant for life.

Joan didn't think the vows made to God were binding, because she wasn't sure she believed in God. So she tried to make up for the hurt she felt over her failed marriage by going out with several men, determined to enjoy herself and find another partner. It was no use. She still felt empty and unhappy.

Joan had scrapped her married name and called herself 'Miss', but her boss knew that she was married. One day she told him she was dreading a meeting with Bernard to complete the division of their property. Bernard had drawn up what she regarded as a very complicated scheme and she resented it. Unknown to her until later the boss, who was a strong Catholic, spent all night in prayer for the couple.

In the meantime, Bernard brooded over Joan's dislike of his scheme. Through his association with a caring group of people who spoke to him of God's love, he experienced a change of heart. So he drafted a new scheme. Joan signed the new scheme straight away, somewhat puzzled that it was so favourable to her. 'How did it go?' her boss asked. 'Quite well,' she replied.

Encouraged by her boss, Joan went to a Catholic Renewal Conference. She had never been to anything like it, and the warmth of the love impressed her. When called to prayer, a thunderbolt of a thought struck her so forcibly that she turned to see if the person behind her had spoken it. 'Go back and ask for forgiveness.' When it came again, she looked up at the ceiling and said, 'If it's you, God, forget it. No way am I going to do that!' She was challenged by the visiting speaker, a Franciscan priest, who said it was impossible to truly love someone whilst harbouring a deep resentment, even hatred, towards someone else. She went to see Bernard.

He was staggered by her apology, and said it was he who should be asking for forgiveness. From that point on, they knew God was asking them to try and make a go of their marriage, even though it seemed he was asking the impossible.

Two strong-willed characters, used to having their own way, are bound to run into trouble when they marry. Bernard and Joan still experienced this, but God was faithful. Through him they found a way of avoiding turning minor clashes into all-out war. When they got up against each other, they asked God to show them a way out of the difficulty, and to take away their resentment. Bernard began to learn what it means really to love someone.

They have found a new richness in their marriage, and now have five children. They are even grateful for the painful times they went through as their faith has deepened and they have been able to help other couples in difficulties and give them new hope. In March 1994 they celebrated the fifteenth anniversary of the renewal of their marriage vows.

QUESTIONS

1. What is a vow? Do you know any other marriage vows? Name them.

2. What does 'forgive and forget' mean?

3. What do you think it means 'really to love someone'? How had Bernard already started to do this?

'Don't let my parents split up'

Jill and Melvin had been married for thirteen years and were desperately unhappy. They had married young and had three children, Anne aged 10, James 8, and Emma 6. Melvin had a poor relationship with his in-laws. He felt they were too critical of him and that Jill always seemed to be on their side.

Jill's problems weren't limited to her marriage. Her parents were also unhappy and on the verge of divorce, so they had no time to listen to her.

Melvin didn't seem to care or understand. 'He had had such a stable home life,' said Jill. She felt as though Melvin and his family looked down on her and her family – especially Melvin's mother.

The situation continued to deteriorate, until the arguing between Melvin and Jill became continual. This upset the children, but Melvin and Jill didn't really notice this; they were too concerned with their own feelings.

Melvin started to look elsewhere for comfort. He became attracted to a young woman. He felt justified in this because he believed his marriage to Jill was now valueless. Jill sensed that there was trouble brewing. Melvin became sullen and didn't laugh any more.

About this time a neighbour, who was a probation officer, asked Melvin to help out one evening a week, working as a volunteer with young offenders. As he came to know them, he realised that they were lacking understanding and love. 'What of my own children?' he thought.

Things continued to get worse, with more rows. The children were unhappy and Melvin was threatening to leave.

Jill was taking medication prescribed by her doctor for nerve problems and epilepsy. She had become very depressed, to the point where suicide seemed to be the only way out. She had no one to turn to. Melvin didn't love her, and the children's lives were on the same unhappy path as her own childhood. Neither the psychiatrist nor the marriage guidance counsellor had helped, and all the doctor said was, 'Keep taking the pills.' She decided she would do so, all in one go, to get out of the misery.

One night she cried out, 'If there's a God up there, and you have a Son, I need him now.' She had not had a Christian upbringing and only knew what she had been taught in school. She said the only prayer she knew, the Lord's Prayer. The response came quickly, a strong warning not to take the pills. Jill cried bitterly, put the pills away, went to bed and slept, something she hadn't done for quite some time.

When Melvin awoke next morning, Jill was gone. 'Where is your Mom?' he asked his children. 'Gone to church,' was the reply. 'Well, if anyone needs it, she does,' thought Melvin. All was quiet when Jill came home.

Jill started to attend church regularly; the hymns and prayers helped her and the Bible readings were comforting. A peace was beginning to grow inside her. It didn't last all the week, but she found herself looking forward to Sundays.

Melvin was suspicious of the change in her, but he was grateful for a more peaceful existence. He had been brought up in the Christian faith when he was young, and was asking himself if perhaps it was for him after all. He thought again about the young offenders and his own children. This made him feel uncomfortable. He thought too about his feelings for the young woman and how he had justified himself by Jill's behaviour.

A calm was beginning to come in the household. The children sensed the change and became a little more relaxed and outgoing. They joined Guides, Brownies and Boys' Brigade at the church. 'Family service this Sunday, Daddy. I'm carrying the flag for the Brigade. Will you come?' James asked one day. Melvin attended with his family and found himself challenged.

Jill realised that for too long she had blamed Melvin for everything and that changes were needed in herself. Early morning prayer-times helped, not only praying but listening too, and writing the thoughts down. One important thought she had was that because Melvin had stopped loving her it didn't mean she had to stop loving him; she must love Melvin more, not less. The children too needed more love and attention. 'Sorries' had to be said to all concerned, including both sets of parents. The relationship between Jill and her mother-in-law began to develop into one of love and understanding.

James told his parents, 'I knew you wouldn't split up and divorce because I asked Jesus to help you when you were so unhappy.'

God has continued to work in the lives of the whole family, in the joys and sorrows, bringing healing and understanding.

Jill has had only had one major epileptic fit since then. With the doctor's help she slowly reduced her medication and now needs only a small amount to keep her epilepsy stable.

The family all take an active part in the lively Anglican church. Jill has a counselling ministry through which she has witnessed many healings in people's lives and relationships.

Melvin, who has given us this story, says, 'Christ is now the head of the household: through the gift of his Holy Spirit he continues to guide us.'

QUESTIONS AND TASKS

1. You are Emma or James. Describe or dramatise a scene at the meal table: (a) before, (b) after the reconciliation of Melvin and Jill.

2. To how many people did Melvin and Jill have to say 'sorry'?

3. What do you think it means to become a Christian?

4. If Christ becomes the 'head of the household' what difference could it make in matters of discipline, finance, communication?

'Now I call him brother'

Alec grew up on a farm in Rhodesia. He used to enjoy going around with his Dad in his truck, helping with the harvesting and feeding the pigs. He often joined the African boys in their play.

At the age of seven he was sent to boarding school, despite loud protests. In April 1964 his father, Ian Smith, became Prime Minister of Rhodesia. Life changed dramatically for Alec at home and at school. The family moved into the huge Prime Minister's residence when he was twelve. In the evening Dad would come in for supper and then go out or work in his study.

At school some boys began sucking up to him, while former friends fell away. To them he was no longer Alec, but Ian Smith's son. To prove that he was no different from anyone else, Alec joined in with the crowd and enjoyed getting drunk. His school work suffered and it was decided he should live at home, under parental discipline, and attend school daily. But the parents were rarely at home. One weekend when they were away Alec held a huge party. The noise was so terrific that neighbours a quarter of a mile away complained.

After leaving school, Alec went to a university to study law. He was in for a shock. Things he had thought to be wrong were accepted as right. Belief in God was discounted by political theorists. He and other students felt lost, and turned to drugs. He had almost lost contact with his parents.

All young men had to serve for one year in the Army at that time. Because he was a student Alec should have been exempt. When he received his call-up papers, he knew this must have been his father's doing and was furious. He hated his military service.

When he was discharged from the Army, Alec resumed his hippie life. He was completely hooked on drugs and started drug-pushing and smuggling. On his way back from Mozambique, loaded with drugs, he got caught by the police. The newspapers picked up the story. The headlines ran: 'Premier's son on drugs charge' 'Smith's son smuggles hashish'.

It was very embarrassing for his parents. Alec felt more alienated from them than ever.

After seeing two musicals, *Jesus Christ, Superstar* and *Godspell*, he began thinking about Jesus. Then a strange thing happened. He had a favourite spot where he would go to watch the sunset and enjoy a 'trip' – a drug-induced experience. One evening when driving back he heard a voice apparently coming from the back of the car. 'Go home and read the *New Testament*,' it said. He looked round, but no one was there. For two days he tried to forget the voice, but couldn't. Then opening a drawer he found a Bible, picked it up and was gripped by what he read.

One day an acquaintance he hardly knew invited him to go to his church. The invitation intrigued him, and he said he'd go the next Sunday. As the time came, he got scared and tried to get out of it. At last he went to the student union and began drinking. An old friend, another hippie, joined him. 'What are you doing here?' asked Alec. 'I'm on my way to church,' was the reply. 'Why don't you come?' It was the very church he had been avoiding, but the friend insisted and they went along together.

The place was packed. People were clearly enjoying themselves, clapping their hands and singing. Suddenly Alec had a vision. He saw Jesus standing with outstretched arms. He knew that Jesus was asking him to give his life to him. 'No! No! No!' he said inside himself as he ran out of the church. For two weeks afterwards he felt empty; he had been given his chance and rejected it. Then one morning he awoke feeling at peace. God was giving him another chance. He got down on his knees and said 'Yes' to God. From then on he felt a new person.

Alec's relationship with his family became quite different. He began to love and appreciate them more. His parents had never stopped loving him.

He looked at what was happening in his country with new

eyes. The conflict between the black nationals and his father's government was deepening. A terrible war of hatred was tearing Rhodesia apart. How could the bitter divisions and hatreds be healed? Alec became sure that God had a plan.

Then he met a group of people from all walks of life and from different churches, some black, some white, drawn together through the work of Moral Re-Armament. The one thing they had in common was the conviction that God, through the power of the Holy Spirit, could bring about changes in the lives of individuals and of nations. A political solution alone could not bring about lasting peace. There had to be real healing between black and white, tribe and tribe.

Alec and his new friends met frequently to pray and talk things over. It became clear that they should organise an international conference to be held in six months' time. Politicians, business people, farmers, tribal chiefs and members of the African National Council poured into it. Some prominent white men apologised for their past racist attitudes. Some blacks witnessed to God's power to put their hatred of whites aside. Alec said, 'I am deeply sorry for my past selfish life-style . . . and I have committed myself to finding a solution for my country, to building bridges of reconciliation and showing the rest of Africa that black and white can live together.'

Sitting in the conference was a Methodist minister, Arthur Kanodereke. He had been cruelly tortured for his support of black guerillas. When Alec began speaking, Arthur's face was like a thundercloud, but it began to soften. He said afterwards, 'I felt my hate die away.' Later he invited Alec to speak at his church. This took courage. Arthur said, 'I'd like to introduce to you the son of the man I hated most. Now I call him brother.'

From then on the two men worked together. They talked with many people and hardened attitudes began to change. Through his friendship with Arthur, Alec began to realise how deep his own prejudice against blacks had been, and his eyes were opened

52

to an Africa he had never seen or understood. Alec took Arthur home to meet his father. After talking with him Ian Smith said, 'If all black nationals were like him, I'd have no trouble in handing the country over tomorrow.'

Fighting and mistrust continued for a long time, but eventually there was a breakthrough. Elections were to be held in which all would participate. Although the blacks did not think this would be fair, and the whites feared violence, they were held without any trouble. When it seemed certain that Robert Mugabe would become Prime Minister, Alec persuaded his father to meet him secretly the evening before the election results were announced.

Next day Robert Mugabe, now Prime Minister of the newly independent country of Zimbabwe (formerly Rhodesia), said on television, 'Our new nation requires of everyone to be a new man, with a new mind, a new heart and a new spirit . . . that must unite and not divide.'

The two rival guerilla forces and the white army, their former enemy, were given a retraining programme to form into one national army. Alec Smith became one of the army chaplains and continued the work of reconciliation.

QUESTIONS AND TASKS

1. Illustrate any incident from Alec's life or describe it in writing, beginning: 'My name is Alec.'

2. What part did people, a book, prayer, play in Alec's change?

3. What were some of the results of that change?

4. Why do people become addicted to drugs? Do you think it is important to value people for what they could be, rather than what they are?

6. DESPAIR AND PRAYER

Crises in life can lead to deep changes of outlook and belief. These three stories are about people who reached a point of despair not only about their situations but about themselves.

As they reviewed their lives their consciences began to work. They had a sense of God meeting them at their point of need, and were open for what he might have to say. They began to get a new hope, a new purpose for their lives.

Several discussions with students about God's communication with us led to the questions of conscience and prayer.

> **Conscience is something that comes from inside myself. It's like a little voice. I imagine that I have a good angel and a bad angel inside me. Actually, I've got a bad streak. I know when to stop now.**
>
> Marie, 13

> **My personal idea of God is someone you turn to for support and consolation whenever you need to.**
>
> Derek, 13

> **If I pray and something comes right, God is confirming the relationship.**
>
> Peter, 17

> **If you have asked friends to help you and they have prayed for you, is that God? Has his influence come into the process?**
>
> Trevor, 17

STORIES   Jane and her Drink Problem
                            'I'm innocent'
                            Escape to Live

54

Jane and her Drink Problem

Jane was adopted. She lived with her new parents in a village in the south of England. She loved her adoptive father, but not her mother, who treated her very harshly at times.

She had been taught about God and believed he loved her until one day when she was ten she found some money hidden away and stole it. She was dealt with severely and believed God didn't love her any more, as she was too bad. That made her despair of herself.

Jane was clever and stayed on at school until the sixth form. Then she went to pieces when her father fell ill and died. She had already started drinking when she was fifteen. She stole and lied to get money for drink and was soon drinking quite a lot, without any immediate effects. Black-outs and loss of memory came later.

After a violent row with her mother, Jane packed her belongings and left. She went to a large city to be with a boy she knew. She found a job, had several brief sexual encounters and became pregnant. She continued drinking occasionally.

When her baby was born, Jane went to live with a young couple who regularly took in and cared for unmarried mothers and their babies for a short period. They were very kind and supportive. While living in their home she read an article which said, 'God has a plan for your life.' An address was given through which she met some people to whom she felt she could talk freely.

One thing, however, which she did not tell her new friends was that she had a drink problem. Afraid, perhaps, that they would find out, she packed her bags and moved away, leaving no address or explanation. She did not contact them for a long time, but she never forgot one thing they used to say to her, 'If you listen, God can speak to you.'

Jane was now twenty-two and her son was four. They were housed in a flat. She had started drinking very heavily and neglected her son. The electricity was cut off as there was no money to pay the bill, and she was evicted from the flat. Then Jane met and married Alan, another heavy drinker. He was talented and worked in the entertainment industry. Neither of them realised they were alcoholics, thinking this term applied only to drunken old men sleeping rough on park benches! Their family had increased by three and they couldn't cope with the financial responsibility of running a home. They lived in a dream-world and had no idea how to care for their children, for each other or anyone else. Alan began to treat Jane very badly. She felt full of self-distrust and self-loathing.

It was time to get expert help. So Alan went along to Alcoholics Anonymous, A.A. for short (see page 100). This organisation has existed for many years in most cities in England and America. Jane went to a support group for friends and relatives of alcoholics. When she realised how deep was her own craving for alcohol, she too joined the A.A.

Alan put up a great fight against his addiction, but he slipped back sometimes. When he eventually died he had been sober for the previous eight months.

Jane found help from the twelve-point programme of the A.A. The first step was to admit that she was powerless over her addiction to alcohol and that her life had become unmanageable. Next she came to believe that a Power greater than herself could restore her sanity. The third step was to make a decision to turn her will and her life over to the care of God, as she understood him. She took stock of her life, along with a trusted friend, to find out where she had gone wrong. She realised that all her life she had been desperately lonely and afraid, angry too with both her mothers. Jane gave these things to God, asking him to help her, and straightaway the hatred of her mothers vanished. She made amends, where she could, to people she had hurt over the years. There were practical things to put right too. She and her home needed tidying up, and she took more care of the children, who had suffered from the tensions and uncertainties in the home.

An alcoholic tends to be lonely, obsessive and addicted. Jane smoked as many as seventy cigarettes a day. With the help of God she conquered her addictions and became a different person, and in turn was able to help others. She has lectured on addictions in schools and continues to help and strengthen those still struggling with their addictions to alcohol.

Jane had made contact with her adoptive mother, and when she heard that she was dying of cancer, went to look after her. This was difficult, but God honoured her many prayers and took away her fears.

The very first night many things from the past came out, on both sides. They even talked about Jane's natural mother, a taboo subject before. Her adoptive mother spoke of her bitterness at not being able to have a child of her own. Her hard attitude had gone, and she was just so gentle. There was a total reconciliation.

Jane came to realise God's love for her. He hadn't just loved everyone else in the world and left her out! She still seeks through prayer and listening to improve her conscious contact with God and finds that he does indeed have a plan for her life, and for every day.

QUESTIONS AND TASKS

1. What is wrong with being an addict? Make a list of addictions you know about.

2. How could talking to a trusted friend help?

3. Why was it important for Jane to make amends?

4. Why do you think Jane became an addict in the first place?

For the sake of anonymity the original name has been changed.

'I'm innocent'

'It won't be long now.' Rita Nightingale, an attractive young girl with soft brown hair, sat in the departure lounge at Bangkok airport waiting for the plane to Paris. She had come from Hong Kong where she had met a charming Chinese man named James Wong at the night club where she was a hostess. Night after night he met her after work and took her to dine at expensive restaurants. It was not long before they became lovers. James was so attractive, so generous, and very interested in her family in England.

Rita was homesick at times. She had gone abroad for glamour and excitement, but never felt really happy. Then James had said he must go to Europe and suggested she might like to visit her parents in Blackburn; he would pay the fare and make arrangements. He even bought her three expensive holdalls and gave her money for new clothes.

At the last minute he could not go with her, but left her and the luggage in the care of his friend, Simon Lo. Simon would go with her to Bangkok, where she was to catch a plane to Paris and meet up with James before going on.

Suddenly, a tap on her shoulder. Startled, she looked up. 'I am from Customs; come with me.' It could only be a formality and she smiled as they looked through her luggage. To her horror, large amounts of heroin were found in false bottoms fitted to the holdalls. They questioned her for hours, asking her to sign forms in the Thai language which she did not understand. At her pleading, they took her to Simon's hotel. 'Who are you?' he asked coldly, as they entered his room. She flew at him, sobbing and shouting. The police took her back to the waiting car. They arrested Simon, but later released him.

The cell Rita was put in was dark and dirty, and full of cockroaches. She kept protesting her innocence. 'They all say they are innocent,' she was told. She worried about her mother hearing of her arrest. And what about James, who would be waiting for her in Paris? An older prisoner said, 'Don't you see? He fixed it all.' Oh no! She was deeply hurt, then furious.

British Embassy officials visited Rita and arranged for a lawyer. He promised to do his best and explained the long legal procedure. He warned her that the Thai government was under international pressure to be severe with drug smugglers.

Rita wrote desperate letters home. Her family believed in her innocence and did all they could to help. Her arrest and imprisonment were reported in the British newspapers, and the local paper *Lancashire Evening Telegraph* began a campaign for her release. Their reporter, David Allen, flew out to Bangkok where he saw a video film of her interrogation. Her stunned look convinced him of her innocence. Later the paper paid for her mother to visit her.

Many letters of support poured in and over 200,000 people signed a petition for Rita's release. There were several court hearings. She refused to plead 'Guilty', which would have got her a lighter sentence.

One day two visitors came, Lucille and Margaret, with a present of pineapples. 'We heard about your case,' they said. 'What brings you here?' asked Rita. 'We came because God told us to. He cares about you.' 'God has not done anything for me. If there is a God, he doesn't come in here.' 'But he has, Rita,' Margaret replied. 'He told us to come.' When Margaret talked about Jesus, it was as if he was a close friend.

Rita kept brooding about her future. She was likely to get a fifty-year sentence. She kept wondering how she could prove her innocence, and how to get even with James.

Another visitor came. 'I'm Martha Livesey,' she announced. 'I've come to see you, love, because I'm from Blackburn too.' Rita burst into tears. 'I want to go home . . . I want to go home.' After a few minutes Martha left, giving her a bag.

A turmoil of thoughts went through Rita's mind. Why had it all happened? Why was she in prison? Why did her family have to suffer? Why? Then she went back over the past. Why did James single her out to deceive? Her questions seemed endless.

She opened the bag. Inside was a booklet called *The Reason Why*. It made her think. She had been the victim of the wickedness of others, but also she had been foolish, though she thought herself clever and sophisticated. Her life was in a mess – and so was the world. But God had sent his own Son to live, suffer and finally to die for the selfish human race; through his resurrection he had been victorious over death itself.

Rita began to understand why she had always been restless. God had been missing in her life. He was telling her now that there was real love – his love – which made sense of all human loving.

She must respond, she must talk to God. The words spilled out, 'I'm sorry for the mess I've made of my life. I'm sorry I've not wanted you. Please come into my life and change it.'

God's response came, deep inside, 'Give me your life and I will change it. I love you.'

Rita borrowed a Bible from the prison library. She poured out to God all the things she had never been able to tell anyone before. Her feelings of loneliness went, and she began to see everything differently. As she learned to care for people in many little ways, life became interesting. It might even have been worth coming to prison for.

Then came the trial. Despite the months of hard work by lawyers, Embassy officials and others, a harsh sentence seemed inevitable. Yet Rita had an incredible feeling of peace. She was aware of God helping her not to despair and not to be bitter.

The court was crowded. Jim Biddulph from the BBC was there, with television cameras. The sentence was twenty years. She kept sobbing, 'But I'm innocent.' She would be over forty when released.

'We must appeal,' said the lawyer.

Two prison missionaries gave her a booklet, *The Freedom to Choose*. It made Rita see that she must forgive the prison warden, whom she hated, and also James and Simon Lo. This was not easy; sometimes the resentments came back and she had to forgive all over again. Fears and uncertainties began to take possession of her. The missionaries suggested that each morning she should pray and bring these fears to Jesus. This helped a great deal.

The appeal was dismissed. The only hope left was an appeal to the King of Thailand, but this was unlikely to succeed. Chains of prayer were set up around the world. Then the unlikely thing happened. Eventually the King of Thailand granted an amnesty. Rita had been in prison for three years.

Rita Nightingale wrote a book about her experiences called *Freed for Life*. Her second book *Freed for Ever* tells of her difficulties in adjusting back home in England, despite the warm welcome from family and friends. Eventually she found joy and fulfilment in visiting prisoners in England and America for the Prison Christian Fellowship. She married happily and had a baby son.

QUESTIONS AND TASKS

1. Draw one incident from this story and write a caption.

2. Imagine you are one of Rita's visitors. Describe the visit, including Rita's reaction to it.

3. How did books help in her communication with God?

4. Rita had every cause to be furious with the boyfriend who planted drugs on her. Why was it important to forgive him?

Escape to Live
A story from the Second World War

It was May 1941. In Crete battles were raging between the Germans and the Allies for control of the airfield. RAF fighter pilot Edward Howell lay in a pool of blood, covered with flies. All his aircraft were lost. In fierce fighting on the ground he was seriously wounded and left for dead where he had fallen. But for a partial tourniquet he would have bled to death.

Between long spells of unconsciousness Edward was tortured by a terrible thirst. He was so helpless that he could not move even a finger. Some German paratroopers came by and he managed to croak 'Water.' They gave him the water from their bottles. Eventually he was lifted on to a stretcher and flown to Athens as a prisoner-of-war.

His left shoulder, which was shattered, was operated on and the severe wounds in his right arm bandaged. Both arms were set in plaster, so he had to have everything done for him. He was very weak and in great pain, and few thought he would survive.

After five months he was among the last group of prisoners to be moved north to Thessalonica on the way to Germany. It was a very severe winter so the move was delayed until spring. Edward's health deteriorated and he was taken to a prisoner-of-war hospital nearby. Here his health improved. He began to walk and feed himself with his left hand. His right arm remained useless, with an open wound which refused to heal. He felt helpless and hopeless. All that he most valued seemed to have gone. What had he to live for?

Edward had been brought up to believe in God, but when he went to university he abandoned his belief. He wanted to run his own life without reference to God. So he had chosen to go his own way, regardless. One night he had an experience which transformed him. Unable to sleep, he lay in the hospital bed reviewing his life. He had been thoroughly self-centred, ignoring the needs of others. Often he had been dishonest, mean and selfish. Accepting the truth about himself made him deeply ashamed. Then he remembered what his brother David had told him years before: 'If you really want to become different, hand over your life to God. He will change your motives and behaviour and give you a wonderful new life, if you trust and obey.'

In his despair Edward prayed to God, 'If you are there and will accept me, I will be your man from now on.' It was as if a light had been switched on. The words 'God is love' suddenly became real. He felt in personal contact with God for the first time. It was an indescribable and wonderful experience.

When he awoke next morning he wondered if it had all been a dream. No! His new joy was still there. Other people seemed different, even the Germans. Then he realised it was he who had been changed.

After this Edward began each day by opening his heart to God and asking for his direction. He would get quite simple thoughts like what to say to his fellow prisoners, when to exercise – a painful and tiring process – and when to rest. Every day he studied the *New Testament*. He often thought about whether or not he should try to escape. In his present condition it seemed impossible. He sought God's guidance and to his surprise God seemed to be telling him it was right to try. It was his duty as an officer and it would be a test of faith.

Towards the end of March all prisoners were told they would be moved by train to Germany next morning. Edward prayed to be shown what to do. He was given a growing belief that now was the time to escape. Half-an-hour after dusk he was to be ready and come to a side door, near to the only place he had noticed it might be possible to get over the outer wall.

Edward knew the task was impossible for him. He was still weak and crippled. The side door was kept locked. There was a sentry a few yards from where he would have to climb. He spoke no Greek and did not know where to go if he did get out. The Greeks were under harsh enemy occupation. He would risk being shot, and anyone who helped him would be shot too. Yet not to take the risk would mean that he didn't trust God enough to obey him. He must go!

As he was preparing, his temperature flared up with all the symptoms of a high fever. Was this a sign that he had misunderstood God's message? The thought came: 'Your illness does not make your escape wrong; it only makes it more difficult. You will have to rely on my power.'

Edward continued to get ready. His cell-mate who had lost a leg had given him boots. A raincoat came from another friend. Socks, clothes and chocolate had arrived from home in a Red Cross parcel.

Dusk came. Edward stepped out of his room into the corridor. Where were the German soldiers? Astonishingly, none were about at that time. His fellow-prisoners tried to dissuade him, but his mind was made up. He went to the side door. It was unlocked! There was a full moon and he could see the sentry about fifty yards away with a gun in his hands. It was now or never!

The Escape

He walked across the ash-covered roadway. It crunched loudly under his feet. Apparently the sentry didn't hear him. Then he climbed up a grass bank to get to the top of the inner wall which led to the main outer wall. The sentry was now quite close, and Edward was easily visible. Still the sentry was unaware.

Edward expected to be able to put one leg up and over the outer wall as he couldn't use his hands and was too weak to jump, but the wall was too high. He prayed again. The answer came, 'You have come at the right time to the right place. There is a way over the wall.'

Edward looked again at the wall and found he could bend over the top, but it was covered with spikes of glass. He took the woollies he had stuffed into his pockets and made a pad over the spikes. Then he put his weight on the pad and lifted his legs, intending to wriggle round so as to drop off feet first. Instead he fell head first! Somehow, he never knew how, he landed on his feet and the pad fell into his bent arms. He was astonished at the miraculous way God had made the escape possible and thanked him with all his heart.

Edward was free, first from himself and now from prison. He went to the wall close to where his friends would be and whistled loudly the well-known tune *Loch Lomond* – 'and I'll be in Scotland before you'! They heard him and realised he was safely out.

What next? Again he prayed. Then he noticed the evening star shining brightly in the east, seeming to invite him to follow. To do so meant going along a busy street where he might be noticed. Yet he felt this was the right way to go, and so it proved. No one stopped him. Later that night, high up on the hill, he saw searchlights and heard dogs bark; as he had taken the crowded street they could not pick up his scent.

Many similar answers to prayer continued throughout his dangerous journey. He made his way eastwards across the mountains heading for Turkey. Edward was rapturously happy and gaining in health and strength. Each day he was befriended and helped by shepherds and villagers who fed and sheltered him at the risk of their lives.

After some weeks a group of twenty Greek officers who were escaping to rejoin the Greek army in Egypt asked Edward to join them, and a fishing boat took them across to the Turkish island of Imbros. They sailed by night to avoid enemy sea and air patrols. From Turkey he was flown through Cyprus to Egypt.

Edward was then flown back to England for a reunion with his family and to have surgery to repair his arms so that he could return to service with the RAF. Home was the end of that adventure and the beginning of a fascinating lifetime aimed at following God's leading. He had escaped not only from prison but from himself into a radically different way of life, guided and empowered by God.

The full story of Edward's remarkable adventure is told in his book *Escape to Live* (Grosvenor Books, paperback edition 1983).

QUESTIONS AND TASKS

1. What part did a) a person, b) a book play in bringing a change in Edward's life?

2. You are Edward. Describe your dilemma about whether to escape or not, outlining the difficulties.

3. Illustrate any episode in Edward's story, with a caption.

4. What steps led to Edward's God-given change of heart and behaviour?

5. Under what conditions does God's guidance come clear? (See Romans 12: 1-2)

7. REACHING OUT

Many countries are suffering from the ravages of war. The world wars not only destroyed masses of buildings but also inflicted lasting damage on thousands. Some still suffer from their disabilities and post traumatic stress.

Now we are seeing the horror of civil wars: the violence and killings and streams of refugees, many of them children whose parents may be lost or dead.

Some ask, 'Does God care? Why doesn't he do something?'

God works, as he always has, through people. These stories tell of three men who have been used by him to help in these very situations. A farmer and his family in the west of England found a unique way of helping bereaved families suffering from malnutrition in a country slowly recovering from civil war. A young Swiss man founded a small religious community which is bringing new hope and reconciliation to people of different creeds and nationalities. Thousands of young people who visit it find a purpose and meaning in their lives. An ex-serviceman unexpectedly began caring for ill and disabled people, and started a Home which led to over two hundred Homes in fifty countries. All these men found prayer as their source of power and direction.

This statement shows the need of reaching out to those of a different religion and nationality from one's own:

> I am a Muslim and have, I suppose, been the target of discrimination and often felt isolated in a mainly non-Muslim country. Being surrounded by persons of other faiths . . . I have widened my horizons and understood others a little better. Yet often I am isolated because of my beliefs and my skin, as if I were not of this planet. Yet I, like most religious people, believe in the glory of

God, God's oneness and God's power. I also believe that worshipping God and practising religion will inevitably permeate through life.

I believe that all the different faiths and methods of worship are varying ways of depicting the same picture. They are all trying to achieve the same goal: that there is someone who will always have time for you and support you.

Ahmed, 13

STORIES

Send a Cow
Brother Roger of Taizé
An Unexpected Life

James 1:27

Send a Cow

Anthony Bush is a dairy farmer living in a 17th-century farmhouse in the West of England with his wife Christina, who is an artist. They and their family are keen Christians and Anthony is a lay preacher.

One day a friend phoned Anthony to say that she had a message for him from the Lord Jesus. It was in three parts. Something unexpected was going to happen. He must not shut the door against it. Then came a message from the Lord, 'I will never leave you nor forsake you.'

Two days later a letter arrived from Africa inviting Anthony to speak at a Festival of Healing in Nigeria. This was quite a challenge for a British country farmer but, because of the phone message, he did not dismiss it out of hand. He talked it over with Christina and they decided he should go. There he spoke every evening at meetings of 30,000 people.

While in Nigeria, Anthony was asked to send cows to start a dairy herd at a college. Not knowing much about African farming conditions, he went to a government farm where there used to be a splendid herd of dairy cows. Now there were very few and they were milked by hand through broken-down machinery for which no repairs were available.

On his return to England, Anthony could not forget this situation. He talked it over with another farmer. Was there anything they could do? They explored the possibility of sending some pregnant heifers, but were advised by a government department that the climate in Nigeria was unsuitable. But it had given Anthony an idea.

Then one day a visiting Ugandan bishop who was interested in farming was brought to see Anthony. As they looked around the farm with its excellent Friesian cows, the Bishop talked about the devastation and malnutrition in Uganda, which had been ravaged by civil war. Most of the good milking cows had been killed and those that remained produced very little milk. Anthony felt certain that the Lord was asking him to do something about it.

In the part of England where he and Christina live, Anthony knew a few farmers who would be interested. The farming families started to meet regularly for lunch in each other's homes to pray and talk things over. Numbers slowly increased. Anthony put to them the situation in Uganda. Every time they met they prayed about it and conviction grew stronger and stronger that there was a plan in the mind of God. From these lunch-time family gatherings came a registered charity 'Send a Cow', which works closely with the Church of Uganda and some relief agencies.

In March 1988 the farming families invited others to join them in sending 25 pregnant Friesian cows to Uganda. Friesians, which are black and white, were chosen because of their high milk yield. When they arrived and were let out, they dashed round and round the field of the Entebbe quarantine farm in sheer delight. After quarantine the heifers were distributed to families trained to look after a cow through the Ugandan Church Rural Development programme. A condition of the gift to a farming family was that the first heifer calf would be given to another family.

Back in the West country, news of the project reached the media and money began to come from many sources. Primary schools adopted the cause and their walls were adorned with the children's drawings of Friesian cows. Secondary schools used 'Send a Cow' as a basis for their studies in Geography and the needs of the Third World. Churches too sent donations.

Many individual people raised money. Here is the story of Mrs Winter, who undertook to raise enough money for one cow, about £700. Mrs Winter, who is of West Indian origin and well-known in her area, lives in St Paul's, a part of Bristol with a large ethnic population. Every year a spectacular carnival is held there.

Money is collected at the carnival for three charities chosen by a committee from the churches. One year Mrs Winter suggested 'Send a Cow' for one. This was agreed. She, her family and friends collected money all along the processions, going in and out of shops and pubs. She still needed more money to reach her target, so every day for a month she went out with her collecting box, showing people a picture of a Friesian cow and talking about the needs of Uganda. The cow she paid for was named Panda because, like all Friesians, it was black and white. She was presented with a certificate outside the Black and White cafe.

Through the efforts of people like Mrs Winter and her family, 'Send a Cow' has greatly expanded. Two hundred and fifty Friesians have so far been sent to Uganda. They travel twenty-five at a time, twice a year, in specially air-conditioned planes. Sheds have already been built for them by the farmers, who are often widows, and their children. Four hundred families have now received a cow or heifer calf. There are two fully-trained vets and twelve assistants, many trained in artificial insemination, who travel round the villages on motor bikes.

The benefit to Ugandan families cannot be over-estimated, for the protein supplied by the milk prevents malnutrition and builds up resistance to disease.

'It all began with a phone call,' says Anthony Bush. The call completely changed his outlook. He believes that we have to change our life-style and make sacrifices for others. 'This is a family project right through,' says his wife Christina. It certainly is, the families of Britain caring for the families of a country in need.

QUESTIONS AND TASKS

1. Draw Panda with her Ugandan family.

2. What response do you think the term 'Lord' implies? Select one or more of the following: allegiance, respect, loyalty, blind obedience.

3. Why has 'Send a Cow' been called a 'grass-roots charity'?

4. How did God show his love for Ugandan families in this story?

Matthew 13:31-2

Brother Roger of Taizé

What is it about Taizé that draws thousands of people to it every year?

Where and what is it?

Taizé is a small village in Eastern France, where Brother Roger founded a small monastic community of seven brothers at the top of a hill. Over the years the number has increased to ninety or more, Protestant and Catholic. Some live and work in deprived areas overseas.

Year by year new developments have taken place, not to a pre-set plan or strategy, but through listening together to the Holy Spirit.

Tens of thousands of people come to Taizé from many different countries. They come to deepen their faith, to pray, to find a meaning for their lives and to meet other people. From here small groups go out to poor parts of the world, living among the people and building trust and reconciliation. Today Taizé has become known worldwide through its large international gatherings in big cities, as well as through the media, books and taped music.

How did it all start? Who is Brother Roger?

Roger was born in Switzerland of a Protestant family. His father was a pastor. While at school Roger went through a period of doubt about religion and was helped by the Catholic landlady with whom he lodged. Urged on by his father, he took a training in theology.

As a young man, at a time when humanity was being torn apart, with deep divisions, he wondered why there were these bitter conflicts, even among Christians. Was there some way in which it would be possible for any one person to understand another completely? Then one day he took a decision. He said to himself, 'Assume that that way does exist. I will try to understand everything about other people, rather than expecting them to understand me.'

His thoughts turned to community living. Over many months they took shape and he decided to buy a house where he and others could live by the teachings of Jesus, and have regular times of prayer. Where should it be? It was 1940 and France had just fallen to the Nazi armies. It was going through much suffering, which would continue after the war. It might need what the community could offer.

He crossed over to Eastern France and made his way to the ancient town of Cluny. There he saw a notice 'House for Sale in Taizé'. He knocked and was told that Taizé is a tiny village to the north, and that the keys were with an old woman who lived there. He cycled some distance along the valley, then turned off onto a rough cart-track which led to the half-ruined village. He found the old woman, who went with him to the house. He told her of his ideas. She said, 'Stay with us here. We are so poor, so isolated, and the times are bad.' This made a big impression on him.

After a visit to Switzerland to consult with his father and friends, he returned and bought the house. The owner, who was destitute, had been praying for a buyer when she heard the news.

He set to work preparing the house and grounds, which had been left untended for some time. Taizé was on the route into Switzerland used by refugees, mainly Jews, fleeing from the Nazis. They would arrive at Roger's house exhausted, hungry and in danger. He welcomed and looked after them. His own life was in jeopardy. Before long he was on the Gestapo list, but was warned in time to escape.

Back in Switzerland, he clarified his ideas for community living and published a booklet. Attracted by this, three young men joined him in his flat. They had regular times of prayer.

After the war Roger returned to Taizé. Others gradually joined him and on Easter Day 1949 seven brothers committed themselves for life to serve Christ in the community.

The first brothers came from two or three European countries. Today they are from twenty countries in Western and Eastern Europe, as well as other continents. Having brothers from Asia, Africa and America has made a great difference to their outlook.

Every year the number of visitors to Taizé grew, and soon the village hall was too small for worship. There were no funds to build a bigger church, but a German organisation, set up to construct buildings as a sign of reconciliation in regions terrorised during the war, undertook the building of a large church in Taizé. The Church of Reconciliation, as it is called, was completed in August 1962. It is open day and night, with times of united prayer three times daily. At the sound of a bell, everyone (brother or pilgrim) stops what they are doing and meets in prayer. A wide diversity of languages is used in the services. It is important that all can hear something in their own tongue. The chants, with melodies long remembered, are an aid to contemplative prayer.

In 1981, during the first European gathering organised by Taizé in London, St Paul's Cathedral, Westminster Abbey, Westminster Cathedral and St George's Catholic Cathedral in Southwark, all wired together for sound, were filled to over-flowing, resounding with these chants.

In Madras no building was big enough for the first inter-continental meeting, so temporary structures were made of bamboo and coconut leaves. Brothers from Taizé, together with many young people, had been preparing for the meeting for over a year. They were helped by Christians of all denominations. Many people came from Japan, Korea, Thailand, Cambodia, Malaysia and Australia. Many Hindus and Muslims were present. Prejudices began to fall away, especially between Tamils and Sinhalese, despite conflicts at the time between elements of the two communities in Sri Lanka.

Visitors

Among the many visitors to Taizé was Mother Theresa who came for days of retreat and prayer in 1976 and 1983. Small groups from Taizé worked for some months in Calcutta with Mother Theresa's helpers.

In October 1986 Pope John Paul II made a visit. Seven thousand young people had arrived to join with the brothers in welcome. The Pope said, 'Today in all Churches and Christian communities, and even among the highest political leaders in the world, the Taizé Community is known for the trust, always full of hope, that it places in the young.'

In August 1992 the newly-elected Archbishop of Canterbury, George Carey, led a week-long pilgrimage of one thousand young people to Taizé.

On arrival, everyone is given an information sheet on which is written, 'As you arrive, understand it is part of the community's vocation to welcome you so that you can approach the living springs of God through prayer, through the silence of contemplation, through searching . . . You have come to find a meaning for your life. One of Christ's secrets is that He loved you first. There lies the meaning of your life: to be loved for ever, to be clothed in God's forgiveness and trust.'

What do some of the young people say about Taizé?

Michael, a priest working in the south of England, said, 'Taizé turned my life upside down . . . It was at that time the only place I could go to where I knew I would be listened to and understood.'

'Taizé is no super-pious place where religion is removed far from reality,' wrote Sue from Nottingham, after her first visit in 1981. 'It is a hard place to be because it demands decisions — maybe only little ones, the next step on your journey — but you come back a different person . . . It is stressed that we must return to our own local communities and put into practice the insights we have gained.'

Anne from Marseilles, France, put it another way, 'Here I discovered that with a tiny seed of faith you can say yes. You can start knowing nothing and succeed in something you could never even have imagined.'

Rachel, from England, wrote, 'Here I discovered that prayer is not only saying words to God; it is also listening. It is consenting to remain in God's presence even when nothing seems to be happening.'

Neville, from Leeds, England, returned home determined to understand and respond to those for whom society has few choices. At one time he had been unemployed for a year. He began working with a local church in setting up a self-help project for the unemployed, working mainly among Bengalis, Vietnamese and Pakistanis.

So the Taizé experience reaches out across the world, inspiring many a spirit-led initiative and meeting the needs of countless individuals.

QUESTIONS AND TASKS

1. Why do you think so many young people come to Taizé?

2. You are a young person writing to a friend after a visit to Taizé. Tell her or him of your experiences there, the friends you made and the difference in your outlook.

3. What do you think is the way to understand another person completely?

4. Illustrate something from the story.

Galatians 5:13-14

An Unexpected Life

Leonard Cheshire is known throughout the world for his Cheshire Homes for disabled people. He is also well-known for his outstanding courage as a bomber pilot in the Second World War, for which he was awarded the Victoria Cross.

In 1945 he was celebrating his brother's release from a prisoner-of-war camp, when the conversation turned to God and religion. Leonard tried to change the subject when a young woman he scarcely knew broke in and challenged him by saying, 'There is a God and you know him.' He could not explain it, but all of a sudden he did know him. Leonard tried to rationalise this later, but became sure it was some kind of mysterious encounter, and that God is always wanting to reveal himself in a quiet, gentle way, perhaps through an inner prompting.

With the end of the war, Leonard found it hard to know what to do. The RAF had given him a discipline and sense of direction. He had seen what can be achieved when men and women are united in pursuit of a common goal. There were many ex-servicemen like him: perhaps they could form a community where by pooling their resources and skills they could help in the rebuilding of post-war Britain. There was an excellent response. With a minimum outlay of capital they acquired Le Court, a large estate with a twenty-five bedroomed Victorian house. Before long the community ran into difficulties and heavy debts, so the scheme was abandoned. Leonard had to wind up the community's affairs and pay off the debts by starting to sell the estate, piece by piece.

In the midst of all this, the phone rang one day. The matron of a cottage hospital was seeking his help over a patient, Arthur Dykes, who had cancer and was beyond further medical treatment. They could not keep him as they had a long waiting list, but he had nowhere to go. Leonard remembered him vaguely as the pig-man at Le Court. He tried in vain to find a place for him, and very reluctantly offered to take him in. There were no amenities on offer, Leonard was unskilled in nursing, and there was no money to pay for help. Arthur was delighted, and felt he had come home. He was very independent, though desperately ill, and Leonard had with great difficulty to help him up the stairs, as he refused to be carried.

One evening Arthur said, 'You are thinking of selling the house, aren't you, Leonard?' 'Yes, I must think about a career and this house is far too large for me.' 'I think,' said Arthur, 'you'll find there are others like me with nowhere to go. If someone comes along, please don't turn him away.'

Leonard couldn't see himself spending his life looking after old, infirm people; he was totally unequipped for it. But things came about as Arthur had foreseen. First he was asked to take in a helpless old lady of ninety-one, then others, until there were nearly thirty residents.

The house was in a bad state of repair, and there was no system or routine. Yet because of this the residents began to find resources and skills in themselves, so that nearly everyone was able in some way to help with the chores. They felt needed and so a happy community came about which, in a sense, fulfilled Arthur's original idea.

A year after Arthur died it became clear that the Home and its finances must be brought under proper control, so Leonard formed a committee. He was alerted to the needs of young people through a boy with a rare disease. The committee had also been asked to cater for young people, so now they were included along with the older ones.

A second Home was started, and soon a third one was to be established, when Leonard became ill with tuberculosis and had to spend two and a half years in a sanatorium. His father and mother persuaded Leonard that it was time to create a charitable foundation. He found it hard to hand everything over, but this released him for what was to become a quite unexpected expansion of his work.

A Scotsman flew in to see him from India. He wanted to do something for disabled people there, perhaps along the lines of the Cheshire Homes. Leonard, still in a sanatorium, promised to visit India when he was fit enough. This visit, two years later, led to many openings, first in India and then in West Africa, Morocco, Jordan and other countries. The initiative always came from local people who undertook full responsibility for financing and administering the homes.

It was in India that he met Sue Ryder. He recognised that she had a sense of vocation and urgency, although he had not heard of her tireless help for thousands of war victims, and her own Homes. Four years later they married. It was not possible to merge their Foundations, but they gave, and give, each other support and have worked together on some projects. They often have to travel long journeys to visit their 264 Homes in 50 countries. They live at the Sue Ryder Foundation Headquarters where their two children were born and brought up, mixing happily with other residents.

What is Leonard Cheshire's source of strength? He has never wavered from the belief in God which came to him in 1945. This was reinforced when Arthur, a lapsed Roman Catholic, regained his faith and became a new person. This led to Leonard becoming a Roman Catholic, which he regarded as the greatest gift Arthur could have given him.

At one time when in Australia a reporter questioned him about his faith, one question was, 'How in a busy life do you find time for prayer?' Leonard replied, 'I pray at moments of opportunity – while going to answer the doorbell or telephone or waiting for the coffee to brew . . . The prayer of total silence is rewarding, not trying to say anything, just being silent in God's presence, enabling him to work inside you and make you able to carry out his will. I try to have at least an hour of silence each day. When you can restrain your wandering thoughts, treat them like background traffic noises, you feel sometimes that you are glimpsing God's plan for you.'

'He has a plan?' asked the interviewer.

'Yes,' was the reply. 'For everybody I think the most important thing in life is discovering what the plan is. You keep searching and the plan unfolds minute by minute as your life proceeds, through people you meet, circumstances you encounter. The search never ends. For instance, I don't know at this moment whether I am following God's plan. He is incomprehensible.'

'Isn't that a discouraging concept?'

'No. One step at a time is enough for me. If I could see further down the road I might not have the courage to walk along it . . . Following his (God's) plan for you may mean you have to face despair and a feeling of total failure.'

Leonard continued, 'Disabled people are blessed with purposefulness. They need to try every moment to make the most of their lives. They eliminate meaningless activity . . . Often the afflicted attain a marvellous peace with themselves. Their achievements strike me sometimes as greater than those of our great men of power and talent.'

In conclusion Leonard added, 'I see life as a journey in prayer, differing as life progresses and different for each person. What may be applicable for me today isn't applicable to somebody else, because he is on a different journey.'

QUESTIONS AND TASKS

1. You are Leonard. Write a letter to an ex-RAF friend explaining your dilemma over Arthur's need of somewhere to live. Outline your own difficulties in offering to look after him.

2. Trace the steps in Leonard's life which led to his life's work.

3. In a busy life, how does Leonard find time to pray?

4. Discuss what Leonard says is 'the most important thing in life'.

5. What is meant by someone else being 'on a different journey'?

8. BEYOND THEIR WILDEST DREAMS

The course of our lives is sometimes determined by the decisions we make when we are young. In school for example our choice of subjects affects our careers.

In these stories two boys, aged fourteen and thirteen, decided to follow Jesus. This meant following his example and teachings and being ready to serve in whatever field opened up.

Right from childhood Jackie too knew there was something she was meant to do with her life.

It would be some years before they found out what God wanted them to do. In two cases it was to go into the unknown, to difficult, dangerous territory and help to bring changes in people and situations with far-reaching results.

Simon, a sufferer from cerebral palsy, took on something nearer home which many people would consider impossible.

All had built up their faith in God and found that what he had in store for them was beyond their wildest dreams.

Here are some of the comments made during a discussion:

> Q. Do you believe God has a plan for your life?
> A. He has a plan for everybody's life.   Roger, 14

> Q. How do you think God reveals himself to people?
> A. Through dreams. God told Joseph in a dream to take Mary and the baby Jesus to Egypt because Herod was having all the baby boys killed.   Mary, 13

STORIES: Dreams
                  Taking a risk
                  'I need you, Simon'

Dreams

Do you think that dreams can have a meaning? Or that God can speak to someone today as he used to do in the days of the Bible?

From childhood Jackie Pullinger had felt that God had a purpose for her life. She assumed this must mean missionary work, probably in Africa, and her idea of it didn't appeal at all. She took up music as a career and enjoyed teaching. But the idea would not go away.

Then one night she had a vivid dream in which her family were all crowded round the dining-room table looking at a map of Africa. In the middle of different coloured countries, a pink one stood out, named HONG KONG, which is not in Africa!

Did the dream mean anything? Jackie was not sure, but felt she had better follow it through. She contacted the Hong Kong government: they had no jobs for musicians. Next a missionary society: she was too young and they did not take anyone under the age of twenty-five.

She prayed about it. Presently the thought came, 'Go. Trust me and I will lead you.'

She talked to a minister, who said, 'If God is telling you to go, you had better go.'

'How can I? I don't know where to go,' replied Jackie. 'All my applications have been rejected.'

'If you have tried all the conventional ways and God is still telling you to go, you had better get on the move . . . If I were you, I would buy a ticket for a boat going on the longest journey you can find and pray to know when to get off.'

This appealed to Jackie.

'It sounds terrific, but it must be cheating because I'd love to do that.'

The minister assured her that it was in accordance with Biblical teaching. Abraham, for example, had left his country and gone out not knowing where he was going, because he trusted God.

'You can't lose if you put yourself in God's hands,' the minister continued. 'If he doesn't want you to get on the ship he is quite able to stop you.'

Jackie counted her savings and booked for as far as the money would take her. She arrived at Kowloon in Hong Kong with just £6. The immigration officer did not want to let her in. She had no job to go to, nowhere to live, and no friends in Hong Kong. Why, the £6 would not last more than three days. Suddenly she remembered her mother's godson in Hong Kong, who was a policeman. That satisfied the official.

Jackie found her way to the Walled City. It was a place full of utter depravity: children on drugs from their earliest years, girls sold or seduced into prostitution, opium dens, thefts, violence and killings. Most of it was controlled by Triad gangs. Jackie saw some of this as she picked her way through the putrid smell of rotten foodstuffs, excrement and stench from thousands of people crowded into narrow alleyways. Yet she felt a tingle of excitement. This is where she was meant to work. Her dream had come true.

The Youth Club

She did not at that time speak Cantonese, and did not know how to communicate with these wretched youngsters. Only God's love could reach them. She must express it through showing she cared, something few had experienced.

Jackie took a job as a music teacher to support herself, and found a room which would serve as a youth club. She bought skate boards, football boots, ping-pong equipment, and organised activities. Thirteen- or fourteen-year olds were the first to come. Gradually she made friends and others came, curious to find out more about this strange English lady. They did not care for the 'Jesus slot' at first, but after a time joined in the hymns.

Ah Ping, who belonged to a Triad gang, which no one was

allowed to leave, often came. One evening he said to her, 'You'd better go and find a nice group of well-behaved students to work with. We're no good. We just muck up all you try to do for us. So why do you stick it?'

Jackie explained, 'I stick around because that's what Jesus did for me. He didn't wait until I got good. He died for me anyway.'

Ah Ping could not believe that Jesus could love someone like him: 'We have to rape and we fight and we steal and we stab. Nobody could like us like this.'

Jackie tried to explain that Jesus could and did love him, while hating what he did. Ah Ping was astounded. He told Jesus he could not understand why he loved him, but asked Jesus to forgive and change him.

Jackie had a feeling she should warn him to watch out for possible danger on the way home and not hang around. Ah Ping felt quite sure he could take care of himself and wandered around a bit. Suddenly seven men jumped out of a dark alley and attacked him, beating him unconscious to the ground. Ah Ping remembered about praying; as he did so his father came down the street and the attackers ran away.

One day Jackie got to the club and found everything smashed up in the most disgusting way, sewage daubed on walls and floor, all the equipment smashed up. Filth from the surroundings outside had seeped in.

All her efforts had gone for nothing. She wanted to sit down and howl. Was this really where God wanted her? She pulled herself together and began cleaning up the place. It took a whole day. Next night the club opened as usual. But her confidence had been shaken and she felt afraid for the first time.

Goko

A young fellow she had never seen before was lounging by the club door.

'Got any trouble?' he asked. 'No, it's fine.' 'Got any trouble –

just let me know.' 'I'm happy to hear that. But who are you?' 'Goko sent me,' he replied abruptly.

Goko was the leader of the Walled City Triad set-up. He controlled all the opium dens and vice in the area. Jackie had never met him but for years she had been sending messages to Goko who never responded.

'Goko said if anyone bothers you or touches this place, we're gonna "do" him.' Despite Jackie's polite rejection of the kind offer, the protector came each evening. He never came in, just stood by the door watching and listening to the boys' spirited rendering of the latest hymn.

Late that evening, when the club was almost empty, Jackie said, 'Now, how about you coming in and praising God?'

'Okay,' he said, without hesitation.

Jackie was astonished. He had the special rank in the Triad of 'fight-fixer' and was very tough indeed. Yet he came inside, praising God at the top of his voice – though he had no idea how to sing. Then he began to praise God in a new language. In about half an hour he stopped and Jackie knew he had been completely cured from drug addiction. He had come through the withdrawal as he worshipped.

'This is wonderful,' said Jackie. 'Now you have to lead your gang to make the same discovery for themselves. You can't follow Goko any more. You have to follow Jesus or Goko. You cannot follow both.'

He went back to his gang-leader Goko to tell him that he now believed in Jesus.

Jackie continued to send messages to Goko, asking to meet him. Finally he consented. She could see on his face marks caused by opium. They talked together.

'You and I both understand power,' said Goko. 'I use my power this way,' clenching his fist, 'and you use it this way,' pointing to his heart. 'If my gang brothers get hooked on drugs, I have them beaten, but I can't make them quit. I've watched you and I believe Jesus can. So, I've decided to give the addicts to you.'

'No,' Jackie replied quickly. 'You want Jesus to get them off drugs and then you want them back, to work and to fight for you! They will certainly return to heroin if they follow you.'

Goko thought this over. 'All right,' he said. 'I give up my right to those who want to follow Jesus.' She could hardly take it in. Once someone became a Triad member it was for life. To try to leave was to invite savage punishment, even death.

Over the years Jackie got to know Goko and his family well, and eventually he too committed his life to Jesus.

Jackie found that many who were hooked on drugs wanted to get off them. When they saw that some of their friends had done so, and looked so happy, they too decided to try the way of Jesus. With only a little experience it was virtually impossible to do so, surrounded as they were by all kinds of temptation. So Jackie began hunting for places for them to live, where they could be trained and encouraged. She worked with other Christians.

In time her work has developed, with special centres for rehabilitation and training. It has become known through television and the press. Jackie Pullinger's book *Chasing the Dragon*, which has sold over 100,000 copies, is full of miraculous stories. A further book *Crack in the Wall* gives many case-histories, with magnificent photographs, and outlines the history and possible future of the Walled City.

The changes there are astonishing. The Triads' hold has been broken, families have been reunited, opium dens have disappeared. Instead of being a city of despair and degradation, it has become a city of hope. Drug addicts have poured in from long distances to find a cure and a new life. Many of those already trained are travelling to many parts of Asia to share their experiences.

Today the Walled City no longer exists. In November 1991 police began moving the last residents of its rotting, rat-infested alleys and slum dwellings. By arrangement with the British Government and China, to whom it will belong when the Chinese regain Hong Kong, it has been planned to become a park.

Jackie's work with drug-addicts and others in need goes on. As one of her fellow-workers said, 'We're not about looking after places. We look after people.'

QUESTIONS AND TASKS

1. You are Jackie. Write to a friend as you set out on your journey. Say why you are going and what your feelings are about facing the unknown.

2. Draw or describe what Jackie first saw when she arrived at the Walled City.

3. Why wasn't Jackie put off by what she saw?

4. Why do you think Goko, the dreaded Triad leader, sent someone to protect Jackie after the Club had been vandalised?

Taking a Risk

At the age of fourteen, Berkeley Vaughan made the biggest decision of his life: to follow Jesus. He was at a Christian summer camp and the leaders had, quite simply, told the boys what Jesus meant to them and invited the boys also to give their allegiance to him.

What does it mean to follow Jesus? Some would say it means to follow his example. For Berkeley it also meant that he would follow where Jesus led. He had a sense of calling, or vocation.

As he grew older, he began to sense that he was meant to become a medical missionary, so he began to train as a doctor at St Bartholomew's Hospital, London, where he qualified. He gained experience in many different kinds of medical work, an excellent preparation for what was to come.

A friend working at the Kwato Mission in Papua suggested this as a possibility, and Berkeley applied for a posting. He did not get an immediate reply, but one day the telephone rang: it was the secretary of the British Committee for the Kwato Mission.

'How soon can you leave for Kwato?'

'In two weeks,' replied Dr Berkeley Vaughan, without hesitation.

'Fine, go right ahead.'

He and his family packed up and went. On arrival they discovered there was no proper hospital, no nurses and very few instruments. Dr Vaughan's medical skills and ability to improvise enabled him to carry out many difficult operations successfully and so win the confidence of the local people.

The missioners were from different backgrounds, yet were very united. Their frankness and fun helped Dr Vaughan, or 'Berke' as he became known, to lose his stiffness and reserve. When a decision had to be made they would pray together and wait for direction from God. Action taken on this basis had a way of working out well, often unexpectedly.

At that time many of the islanders were headhunters and cannibals. Their lives were dominated by fear of the Bad Spirits. If a spell was put on a person, he or she would die. It was usual for one tribe to go armed with spears to fight another tribe, coming back with heads as trophies.

As the missioners gained the people's trust, they said to them, 'You believe in the Bad Spirit. Why not listen to the Good Spirit?' As they did so, they would get simple thoughts that brought lasting changes. One man said, 'Killing won't stop until I am willing to leave my spear behind.' Several women stopped beating their children viciously. Quarrels were resolved, and hardened faces became brighter and happier.

They then set about peace-making. This took the form of deputations to villages where old antagonisms were still being nursed, to tell them of the new way of living.

These peace-making efforts were not always successful at first. One village was hostile and suspicious of the overtures of friendship. After a while the community there suffered from crop failures and food shortage. When their former enemies brought them yams and sweet potatoes from their gardens, suspicion melted away.

A big test came when warriors from a neighbouring tribe destroyed a newly-converted chief's garden and burned down his house. The chief went out unarmed to meet them. He was immediately slashed across the chest, but he stood his ground. This so unnerved his enemies that they left. Days later his assailant visited the chief, who welcomed him warmly. Peace came to that area and still holds firm twenty years later.

When Dr Vaughan returned to Kwato for the Mission centenary in August 1991, he found enormous changes. Swarms of children greeted him in excellent English, and the great-granddaughters of headhunters were handling computers with the greatest of ease.

QUESTIONS AND TASKS

1. Where did Berkeley's sense of calling lead him?

2. What changes took place when the people listened to the
    Good Spirit? Give another name for the Good Spirit.

3. How were enemies changed into friends?

4. What united the missionaries from different backgrounds?
    What might unite people of different forms of religion today?

'I need you, Simon'

Simon Hollingworth lives in the North of England. He is a young man with cerebral palsy and is unable to speak clearly. He cannot control his muscles, arms or legs because his brain does not send the correct messages. Palsy is generally caused by a lack of air at birth.

Simon finds that life with a handicap can be very frustrating over quite simple things. Imagine not being able to get a drink when you want one! However, he has wonderful parents who accepted the situation from the start and are very supportive. They help him with things which he cannot do for himself.

Simon took a course in Computer Studies at a Technical College. Now he has a computer with a special square board. He controls it by a switch on either side of his head. He puts his thoughts into the computer, using a word-processing package. He corrects any mistakes, and when he is satisfied with his work he prints it out. He also has a small portable communicator attached to his wheelchair. This enables him to hold conversations. As you can imagine, his study-bedroom looks like a high-tech laboratory!

Simon is happy. He says that his life is full of peace and joy, in spite of everything. At the age of thirteen he had a holiday with his parents in the Yorkshire Dales at the Dales Bible Week. The question was put to him at a youth group, 'Do you want Jesus to come into your life?' He managed to answer, 'Yes.' The leaders of the group laid their hands on his head and prayed for him. He describes how different he felt inside, and says that he has since had a relationship with Jesus that has been 'great'.

He tells of something surprising that happened to him. He heard a voice saying, 'I need you, Simon.' He didn't know what it meant, but remembered it. Then he listened to a talk about using your talents. What were his talents? He could put his thoughts into a computer for other people to read. He decided to return to the Technical College to develop this skill further.

One day he had another message and felt sure that it came from God. 'Simon, you're going to take the Local Preachers' Exam.' In many churches services may be taken by preachers who have passed some qualifying exam, but are not ordained clergymen. Simon knew how difficult it would be for him to prepare for this and to pass it. In the evening of that very day he had a visit from the minister of the Methodist Church to which he belonged. He had come to talk to him about becoming a Local Preacher and said his name had already been put forward. Simon realised that God had been preparing him for this and accepted the challenge.

How can someone who cannot talk conduct a church service? Simon puts the service into his computer just as he wants it to be and then prints it out. It takes him about thirty hours to prepare a service with the sermon, hymns and readings from the Bible all carefully thought out. On the actual Sunday another preacher takes the whole service from Simon's material.

Communicating with people is a complicated business for Simon, but communicating with God is simple. He says, 'I have experienced quite a few ways of God communicating with me, through the Bible, hymns, songs and people. How? That is the difficult bit to actually describe. It is almost like having a telephone inside my head that is connected straight to God. I can get through at any time, day or night, and talk to God as I would to a friend. "Hi God! I haven't much time to praise you right now, but I just want to thank you . . ." for whatever it is, or "Can you guide me through this situation?" Then I just trust God not to let me down. He doesn't.'

Simon continues, 'God communicates with me through a gentle, soft voice that only I can hear. I could be anywhere, from being in bed to being in the middle of a large crowd. The question that is always being asked is: "How can you be sure that it is God speaking to you?" Very simple. At the same time as the voice talks to me I get a warming feeling inside my heart. This is something that only God can give me. It is a very special feeling. If you have never experienced it, then you cannot imagine it. I'd only say that it is a most wonderful, beautiful sensation.'

The last word must go to Simon's mum, Wendy. She adds that Simon is a very happy young man, good, patient, kind and thoughtful. She can talk to him quite easily and discuss things. He seems to be able to assess a situation and offer comfort or advice. She knows quite a few mums whose handicapped children drive them mad, but not Simon.

Of course, she says, he must be very frustrated at times, especially when he sees his brothers, 21 and 23, coming and going as they please. Also, girl-friends, marriage etc. are a difficulty, but he copes very well. If he gets upset about such things he takes them to God and generally feels much better afterwards.

Finally, says his mother, Simon is not perfect. He is just a normal young man with fears and disappointments, but with a great reliance on and trust in Jesus. He has a good sense of humour and enjoys a joke and a laugh.

QUESTIONS AND TASKS

1. Draw Simon at work in his room with his computer. *Or:* You are Simon. Your friend has a spinal injury in an accident. Write to him or her.

2. Why did Simon become a preacher? How does he conduct a church service?

3. Simon is happy. Why?

4. You are Simon. Describe how God communicates with you.

RESOURCES

Books

A God who Acts H. Blamires, reissued 1983, SPCK

Listening to the God who Speaks Klaus Rockmuehl, Helmers & Howard, Colorado Springs, USA, 1990

Does God Speak Today? David Pytches, Hodder and Stoughton, 1989

Escape to Live Edward Howell, Grosvenor Books, 1983 edn.

The King Among Us Barry Kissell, Hodder and Stoughton, 1992

Freed for Life Rita Nightingale with David Porter, Marshalls, 1995

Chasing the Dragon Jackie Pullinger with Andrew Quiche, Hodder and Stoughton, 1980

Grey is the Colour of Hope Irina Ratushinskaya, Hodder and Stoughton, 1988

No, I'm not Afraid Irina Ratushinskaya, Bloodaxe Books, Newcastle-upon-Tyne NE99 1SN, 1986

In the Beginning Irina Ratushinskaya, Hodder and Stoughton, 1990

God's Hand in History (Series), Mary Wilson, Grosvenor Books, 1983. 3. A Rushing Mighty Wind; 4. Builders and Destroyers; 5. The Word and the Sword: Stories from AD 571 to 14th century.

Packs

The Leonard Cheshire Foundation, 26-29 Maunsel Street, London SW1P 2QN. Special Schools Pack with booklets about Leonard Cheshire and the Cheshire Homes.

The Leprosy Mission, Goldhay Way, Orton Goldhay, Peterborough, Cambs. PE2 5GZ. List of videos, slides, filmstrips, literature, posters, leaflets, information sheets, world map, packs.

COPYRIGHT ACKNOWLEDGEMENTS

The poem 'Believe me' by Irina Ratushinskaya is reprinted by permission of Bloodaxe Books Ltd from: *Pencil Letter* by Irina Ratushinskaya (Bloodaxe Books, 1988). The story 'A Hand on my Shoulder' is based mainly on *In the Beginning* by Irina Ratushinskaya, by permission of Hodder and Stoughton.

'I hate this dump' is based on an article in *Renewal Magazine* by Harry Kissell. The story also appears in *The King Among Us*, published by Hodder and Stoughton, who have given permission.

'Doug and his O.C.' is from *Some Soldier* by Douglas Walters (Linden Hall).

'Escape to Live' is based on the book *Escape to Live* by Edward Howell, Grosvenor Books.

'An Unexpected Life' is based on *The Hidden World* by Leonard Cheshire, published by Collins (1981) and an article in *The Australian* newspaper, 14 March 1991, by permission of Frank Devine.

'Escaped as a Bird' is from the booklet *Escaped as a Bird*, by permission of The Leprosy Mission. The poems are from *Souls Undaunted*, published by American Leprosy Missions.

'Dreams' is based on *Chasing the Dragon*, by Jackie Pullinger with Andrew Quiche, published by Hodder and Stoughton, and newspaper articles.

'Experiencing God through Nature' is from *Through Darkness to Light* by W. Heaton Cooper (Frank Peters, Kendal), by permission.

'Now I call him Brother' is taken from the book *Now I call him Brother* by Alec Smith (Marshalls), © HarperCollins.

'I'm Innocent' is taken from *Freed for Life* by Rita Nightingale (Marshalls), © HarperCollins.

'Brother Roger of Taizé' is taken from *The Story of Taizé* by J.L. Gonzalez Balado, by permission of the Taizé Community, France.

For a Change Magazine have given permission for the following stories: 'Money isn't everything' 'Identity Crisis', 'Snowy', 'Don't let my parents split up' (as re-written by Melvin Hartland) and 'Divorce called off.'

We also acknowledge Mrs Patricia Duce for her story 'Moment of Truth.'

We are grateful to Simon Hollingworth and his mother for his story, to which our attention was drawn through an article in *The Methodist Recorder*.

The verses from Psalm 104 are from the Authorized Version of the Bible (The King James Bible), the rights in which are vested in the Crown, and are reproduced by permission of the Crown's patentee, Cambridge University Press.

THE TWELVE STEPS OF A.A.

1 We admitted we were powerless over alcohol – that our lives had become unmanageable.

2 Came to believe that a Power greater than ourselves could restore us to sanity.

3 Made a decision to turn our will and our lives over to the care of God as we understood Him.

4 Made a searching and fearless moral inventory of ourselves.

5 Admitted to God, to ourselves and to another human being the exact nature of our wrongs.

6 Were entirely ready to have God remove all these defects of character.

7 Humbly asked Him to remove our shortcomings.

8 Made a list of all persons we had harmed, and became willing to make amends to them all.

9 Made amends to such people wherever possible, except when to do so would injure them or others.

10 Continued to take personal inventory and when we were wrong promptly admitted it.

11 Sought through prayer and meditation to improve our conscious contact with God as we understood Him, praying only for knowledge of His will for us and the power to carry that out.

12 Having had a spiritual awakening as the result of these steps, we tried to carry this message to alcoholics, and to practise these principles in all our affairs.